He didn't realize they'd reached her apartment until she stopped outside the door and turned to him, her hands playing with each other in that way of hers that he shouldn't already be able to recognize as anxiety.

"Well. This is me." She screwed up her nose. "Um… thanks for this evening. It was…"

He was too close, he realized belatedly. Too close, and too intent. Wholly unable to tear his eyes from her lips, the rise and fall of her chest, which betrayed how shallow her breathing was, or the way her tongue flickered out to moisten her lips as though her body knew what it was doing even if her head didn't intend it.

Before he could think twice, Tak lowered his head, the fleeting sensation of her hot breath on his chin only charging his body all the more, and claimed her mouth with his own.

He knew he was in big trouble in an instant.

She tasted of lust and longing, and pure sensation. All exploding inside him. Like detonating a charge he'd known all along would send him skyrocketing.

He couldn't get enough.

Dear Reader,

What happens when two people find they desire the very thing that, for years, they'd shied away from the most?

My heroine, Effie, is the epitome of a strong, independent heroine. Having never really had a proper childhood, she was pushed and pulled between a frequently lapsing mother and foster homes. Ultimately, she ended up pregnant at seventeen, and at Oxford University complete with her newborn daughter at eighteen.

For thirteen years Effie's life revolves around the two things she absolutely loves: being a doctor and being a mother, with no room for anything—or anyone—else. Other people could only let them down. And then she meets Tak.

For a heroine as strong as Effie, my hero really needed to step up. And who better than a renowned neurosurgeon who is also compassionate, and who practically raised his three younger siblings with little input from his absentee parents?

But Tak has his own emotional obstacles and vulnerabilities. His life now is all about enjoying the carefree existence that was denied to him as a child. Exactly what Effie doesn't need!

I had a great deal of fun seeing how Effie and Tak's story unfolded, and I truly hope you enjoy reading their story as much as I enjoyed writing it.

Charlotte x

A SURGEON FOR THE SINGLE MOM

CHARLOTTE HAWKES

HARLEQUIN® MEDICAL ROMANCE™

ISBN-13: 978-1-335-64151-9

A Surgeon for the Single Mom

First North American Publication 2019

Copyright © 2019 by Charlotte Hawkes

www.Harlequin.com

CHAPTER ONE

'REALLY? *THIS* IS what you dragged me down here for?' Talank Basu pressed his shoulder against the doorjamb of the hospital's resus department and rolled his eyes at his kid sister. 'I expected some medical emergency, not a schoolyard blind date request.'

'Oh, relax,' Hetti snorted, in a way that no one else talking to him would ever have dared. 'I'm not asking you to marry the woman—just take her to the hospital ball as your plus one.'

'No.'

'Please, Tak? Effie's new to the air ambulance job, and new to the area, and what's more she's really nice. But she has already fended off advances by at least four single doctors and two nurses that I know about, so going alone to the gala would be like painting a bullseye on her back. She could use a bit of support.'

He grinned, unable to resist his habitual teasing of her. 'Ah, *now* I understand. She's another one of your waifs and strays, is she, Hetti?'

'Stop it.' She swatted him good-naturedly. 'You're as bad as Mama. You know *she* wouldn't know compassion if it walked and swamped her in a massive cuddle.'

'Don't disrespect her, Hetti.' Tak frowned automatically.

But instead of backing down, his sister held her ground, narrowing her gaze. 'Why does she always get a free pass with you, Tak? *Still?* We're not kids any more, so you don't have to protect us from who she really is. You sacrificed your entire childhood practically raising Sasha and Rafi and me, being Mama and Papa all rolled into one just to shield us from our parents' inadequacies. Papa was off having his never-ending affairs, and Mama… Well, you know. And that was *before* Baby Saaj.'

Tak didn't bother answering. It wasn't worth the argument. Their parents weren't worth the argument.

Over Hetti's shoulder he could see people milling about, waiting for the next trauma victim to come in. A rare calm before the proverbial storm. The helicopter was only a few minutes out now, and Hetti had got her team together and all the equipment she thought they might need. Now it was just a matter of waiting, and soon the place would be a flurry of activity again.

'Anyway…' Hetti shook her head as though dislodging the argument. 'Effie isn't one of my *"waifs and strays"*, as you so indelicately put it. She was an A&E doctor with me back when I was at Allport Infirmary last year. Turns out Effie has landed herself a plum role on the air ambulance across this way, too.'

'Air ambulance? She must be particularly good.'

'Oh, she is.' Hetti nodded. 'Effie was always exceptional. Noticed things other doctors missed... knew stuff even senior consultants might not know. It was no wonder the air ambulance snapped her up. Even *you* might be impressed.'

'If you're that taken with her then why don't you make her *your* plus one?'

For a moment it looked as though Hetti might want to say more, but then she sucked in a deep breath and grinned back at him in that disarming way of hers that he recognised from when she was a toddler.

'Well, I would, but I'm on call that night,' she shot back instantly, making Tak smile. 'And, no, before you say anything, I *don't* want you to get that changed for me, because then it will mean some other poor sucker who hasn't got a medical god for a brother will end up missing out on the ball instead.'

'Your choice.' Tak shrugged. 'But I told you—I'm going to the ball stag. Although right now I'm going home.'

He should have gone ten minutes ago—well, technically he should have gone three hours ago. However, he'd wanted to stay with his last patient a little longer, and his neurology emergency department had been busier than usual for the time of night.

And now he was here. Because Hetti had asked him to be and because, doctor in her own right or not, she was always going to be his baby sister.

If he'd known Hetti's call wasn't about a patient but about dating he wouldn't have bothered. Especially when she was giving him grief. Like right now.

'Wow, the rumour mill will *love* that. Eligible bachelor Tak Basu attends one of the highest profile events of the year alone? Congratulations. I don't think you could have come up with a better way to stir up the already feverish interest in your love-life, whilst simultaneously encouraging Mama to push you towards an arranged marriage of her preference.'

'It's precisely *because* of those reasons that I'm going alone,' Tak growled—not that it had much effect on his unperturbed sibling. 'I've had enough of being potentially married off to every woman I speak to, let alone date.'

'Only because you'd rather be married to your career. The King of Awake Craniotomies— determined to be better than all the rest of us who want such humble things as relationships, and love, and someone to share their life with.'

'You're enjoying this, aren't you? I never said I was better than anyone,' Tak pulled a face.

'No, but I know you think it. Still, as someone

who is *actually* allowed to love you and want the best for you, I have to warn you that if you attend the gala alone then, despite your intentions, it will look like an advertisement for the fact that you're shockingly single right now.'

'Well, it isn't.'

'*I* know that. But every woman within a hundred-mile radius who fancies her chances is going to be beating down your door. And that's a conservative estimate. Pretty stupid for an intelligent guy.'

He laughed despite himself. 'So, let me get this straight. *Now* you're saying you want me to take some new trauma doctor to the ball for *my* benefit?'

Hetti wrinkled her nose. 'I'm saying you and Effie could be the perfect foil for each other. Neither of you wants a relationship, but you both need someone to keep would-be suitors at bay. And to buy you some time with Mama and the various so-called aunts who have a whole host of potential brides for you all lined up.'

'Yes, this Effie woman might *say* she doesn't want a relationship, but she will. They always do.'

'Geez, big-headed, much? Watch you don't get stuck in the doorway on your way out, won't you?'

Hetti thumped him hard in the arm. Or at least she tried to.

She shook her hand and grimaced. 'My God,

they're right. You really *do* have the body of a PT instructor rather than a doctor. No wonder you're so ridiculously arrogant.'

'Not arrogance,' Tak hunched his shoulders. 'At least not intentionally. It's just fact. No matter how clear I try to be at the start that I'm not in it for a relationship which is going to lead to marriage down the line.'

'Well, not this time. I've met her, and I've seen what she's like with every guy who has tried to flirt with, bar none. She totally shoots them down. Nicely but firmly, no hesitation. Trust me—she is definitely not going to change her mind about wanting a relationship any time in the next lifetime or so.'

'I don't have to trust you.' Eyeing the clock, Tak began to make his move. 'I'm not doing it. Even for you, Little Hemavati.'

She swatted him, laughing. 'Only Mama calls me Hemavati. Just like she calls you Talank. It's her twisted way of trying to show she's in control. But at least wait and see Effie. You never know. You might actually like her. She's focussed and driven—just like you. And she's also pretty stunning.'

'I'm going now.'

Tak slung his bag onto his back and prepared to head out into the corridor just as the double doors on the other side of Resus banged open and the air ambulance crew burst through with their patient. The new doctor with them had to be this Effie person.

Suddenly he realised he'd seen her once before. A couple of months ago when she'd brought in a forty-eight-year-old head injury patient—Douglas Jacobs, who had taken a tumble down a rocky hillside.

'This is Danny, a male cyclist in his twenties,' the young woman announced clearly, expediently, her eyes moving quickly across the resus team, taking in the faces and commanding them with ease. 'About one hour ago he was travelling at approximately twenty-five miles per hour when a car pulled out of a side road in front of him. Danny tried to swerve but hit the car and was seen to be thrown about three metres into the air before striking the ground with some force.'

Tak lowered his bag again, his attention focussed on the new doctor. He couldn't have said what made him stay. Or perhaps he just didn't want to acknowledge it.

Hetti had been right—although neither of them had realised it. Dr Effie Robinson had indeed impressed him. Along with Douglas Jacobs their patient.

'He was wearing a crash helmet but it shattered on impact. Witnesses say he was unconscious for possibly ten seconds. On arrival GCS was nine.'

There was nothing unusual in any of this. Not the patient, not the injuries, not the doctor. So why was he so transfixed? Watching her command the team in her bright orange flight suit, with her glossy hair—a rich, deep red colour—scraped back so severely and twisted so tightly into a bun that it made his eyes water just looking at it?

Last time he'd seen her but hadn't paid attention. He'd been too focussed on his patient. But this time it wasn't *his* patient. And his attention was all on her.

Why? Because she had red hair and blue eyes? Unusual, but hardly unique. So...what?

There was nothing to soften her appearance—not even a hint of make-up. Yet there was no doubt that she was beautiful. And something else—something he couldn't pinpoint, something innate that spilled out from those icy blue eyes. Despite himself, Tak found he was staring, caught up by her and helpless to do anything other than stop and listen.

She barely needed to pause and check her notes. Words flowed smoothly whilst her control of the situation was flawless. He had seen plenty of efficient, skilled air ambulance doctors but she stood out—just as she had a few weeks ago.

There was no reason he should be edging closer, as though he was a latecomer to the team. Her gaze took in the team again, and then she lifted her eyes and connected with his.

Everything stopped. Any thoughts in his head

evaporated, leaving…nothing. It was like nothing that he'd ever experienced before.

So this was Effie.

He stared, unable to look away, and then, incredibly, she blinked once and moved on to the rest of the team. Her voice as steady, and as clear, as even as before. Whilst *he* felt, by contrast, as though his chest had just been belted by the downdraft from a set of helicopter rotor blades. It was an unfamiliar experience.

'He has been intubated and has a right thoracotomy with a flailed segment. Top-to-toe injuries: closed head injury, a six-centimetre right temporal laceration, right clavicular fracture, suspected dislocated shoulder, suspected multiple rib fractures, right thoracotomy and a pelvic splint was applied. He's had morphine and midazolam for sedation and was stable during transfer. Immediate needs are further assessment and imaging to check for internal organ damage.'

She wrapped things up neatly, her gaze steady.

'Okay, we're going to need a whole-body CT, but he isn't stable enough yet to take for imaging.' Hetti stepped in smoothly. 'Allison, what's his BP and heart-rate?'

Effie stepped back to allow the team to take over, nonetheless still on hand to answer any further questions. It was testament to both teams that the handover was seamless, and Effie was soon completing her final paperwork.

Whilst he still stood there. Still watching her. His brain still struggling to get back into gear.

The only thoughts rattling around his head now were echoes of Hetti's words to him. Her ludicrous suggestion which wouldn't have been out of place in a school playground.

And yet here he was, unable to get it out of his head. As though, fittingly, he was nothing but a schoolboy. Yet he'd never been a schoolboy—at least not in that sense of the term.

Even as a teenager he'd been the man of the house. Hetti was right—he *had* practically raised Hetti and Rafi and Sasha. Sometimes alongside their mother—or Mama as Hetti called her—but oftentimes in lieu of her. Especially after Baby Saaj had been born. Ill from the start, his two years on this earth had been a fight every second of every day.

For years Tak had shielded his younger siblings from his father's absences as much as possible. Listening to their mother offer up one convincing excuse after another, praising his father's work as a doctor so they wouldn't realise what a derelict father and cruel husband he was.

The kind of man Tak never wanted to be like.

Hetti might think it was because he was more interested in his career than in having a family, but she'd be wrong. At least she would only be partly right. Forging a career as the kind of neurosurgeon capable of performing a vast array of brain surgeries on awake patients automatically made him the worst kind of unreliable boyfriend. And he was happy with that.

Even so, his career wasn't the whole of it. The whole of it was that he feared being the kind of man whose selfish, self-centred actions hurt any wife, any child, the way his father had hurt them. Time and again. And the truth was that he *would* be that kind of man. However much he abhorred the thought, it was unavoidable. Inexorable. It was in his blood.

Just as it was in Rafi's blood.

Much as he loved his younger brother, Tak wasn't blind to the fact that Rafi was their father all over again. And Tak hated that. Yet here he was. Staring at this doctor as though he'd never seen anyone, any*thing* quite like her before.

It made no sense.

There was something about her which snagged his attention and made him think she possessed a unique quality, even if he couldn't put his finger on what that was. He told himself that he certainly wasn't following the long, impossibly elegant line of her neck, or wondering what that glorious hair might look like free of its rigid net cage, or imagining what lay beneath that less than flattering orange suit.

Still he didn't move.

Once Effie was done with her notes she'd be back to the heli and to her base, ready for the next shout. Which was a good thing. A great thing. It meant he could get past this crazy moment and back to real life.

A life that didn't include his baby sister interfering in his life and picking out potential dates for him, he reminded himself firmly. Least of all dates with a woman like Effie.

Except hadn't Hetti told him that it wouldn't *be* a date? Not in any real sense of the word, anyway. What had she called them…*the perfect foil for each other*? Each of them using the other to keep the world off their back?

It should sound ludicrous. It *did* sound ludicrous. But in between women taking his single status as evidence that of *course* he must be yearning for the perfect wife, and his mother becoming relentless in her desire to see all of her children settled down, even against their will, ludicrous might just work.

It wasn't as though he could simply turn around and tell Mama to stay out of his personal life, much as he might want to. She would always be too fragile, too weak to handle it—their father had made sure of that. And she might not have been the perfect mother, but at least she'd always been *there*.

Hetti was right. He needed a foil. A distraction. *Effie.*

Tak turned back to eye the new air ambulance

doctor again just as she was finishing up her notes.

As if it was meant to be. Effie. *Dr Effie Robinson*. He remembered her name now, from Douglas Jacobs's notes. He narrowed his eyes for a moment.

'Dr Robinson, I wonder if we could have a word? In private.'

CHAPTER TWO

'LET ME GET this straight—you're asking me out on a date?'

Effie was infinitely proud of the way she'd kept any shake out of her quiet voice. The same could not be said for her stentorian heart.

'No. I'm asking you out on a *fake* date.'

'I don't know whether to be amused or insulted.' Her eyebrows felt as if they were somewhere up in the vicinity of her hairline. 'Is this some kind of practical joke? Hazing the new member of staff? Because I can tell you right now—'

He made no attempt to conceal his irritation as he cut her off. 'It isn't. I don't have time for stupid pranks, and I hardly think this would be a particularly funny one even if I did. I need a date for the ball and you fit the bill.'

'There are probably a hundred women in this hospital alone who would jump at your *oh-so-romantic* offer.' Effie felt she'd injected just the right amount of sarcasm into her tone. 'But I am not one of them.'

She wasn't some green doctor, about to go giddy because the gorgeous Tak Basu was talking to her. She'd refused to do that six weeks ago, when one of her first ever air ambulance cases had thrown her a hillside rescue and a man, Douglas Jacobs, suffering from expressive aphasia.

Tak had been the neurological consultant on call. He'd threatened to steal her breath away on sight. But she'd been determined not to let him.

Tall, with archetypal brooding dark looks, he wasn't exactly a playboy, but rumour had it that he had dated some high-profile stunning women in his time.

Well, good for him. But good-looking, arrogant males held little interest for her. Hadn't she been there, done that, and ended up at just turned eighteen years old, heading to Oxford University with a newborn infant in tow?

For the past thirteen years Nell had been her life. She hadn't wanted anything—even her longed-for medical career—as much as she'd wanted to take care of her daughter. But something about this man sent her body's warning system into motion, into an internal flurry, like ants who had just had dirt knocked into their nest.

'I don't think you are remotely *one of them*. Which is precisely why I'm asking you. No jokes, no hazing—just a mutually beneficial arrangement.'

She opened her mouth to reply but no words came.

A fake date, indeed. It should sound insane. Nonsensical. Yet his rich, even tone and neutral expression made it sound utterly plausible. Normal, even. As if a fake date was a completely run-of-the-mill daily event.

Perhaps it was in his world.

Tak Basu—one of the hospital's brightest stars. Talk about an eligible bachelor. His reputation for medical excellence preceded him only slightly more than his brooding good looks and an immorally stunning Adonis physique that would make even the most pious woman ache to sin.

Yet now she realised that not even the most fevered description could accurately convey just how devastating he was in the flesh, or just how paralysing his sheer magnetism truly was.

Every hair on her body felt as though it was standing to attention. Ready to do his bidding—eager, even. It was like nothing she'd ever experienced in the whole of her life.

Then there were the smaller things. Like his big hands, strong forearms, the way he stood as though he owned the world. Or the shock of thick black hair, longer on top than she might have expected, which only added to his already six foot three height. It looked soft and inviting, and it took Effie a moment to realise that her fingers were actually aching with the urge to test it out.

And so she perched there on her stool, pretending she was still working so that she didn't have to turn to him and withstand the full weight of her inconvenient attraction. The fact that he didn't

seem to date much only enhanced his appeal—
and his mystique.

Finally—mercifully—she found her tongue
again. 'What on earth makes you think I want
a fake date?' She flushed. 'Or indeed *any* kind
of date.'

She studiously ignored the little voice in her
head taunting her for engaging with him. Telling
her that had it been anyone else she would already
have declined politely before walking away.

'Isn't that rather the point?' His mouth curved
slightly in what could only be described as a sinful smile. 'If it's a fake date, then it *isn't* really
any kind of date.'

'Semantics.' She pursed her lips. 'Or riddles.
In any case, I've never really cared for either. Just
as I really don't need a date—fake or otherwise.'

Still she didn't make herself walk away. Why
was that?

'I don't understand how I...how a *fake date*...
concerns me.'

And she wanted to understand. Perhaps a little
bit too much. Even if he *was* eyeing her as though
to him she rated as about as intelligent as the av-
erage sponge in the animal kingdom. She could
take offense, but that really wasn't her style. Who
had time in a job like her?

'Hetti suggested otherwise.'

'Hetti?'

'Yes, Hetti. The other Dr Basu.' He jerked his

head towards where his sister and her team were focussed on the cyclist. 'Hemavati.'

Something clicked. How had she missed it before? Probably something to do with the stress of moving house, moving town, moving halfway across the country. And at every step fighting with her thirteen-going-on-thirty-year-old daughter, who hadn't wanted to leave everything she knew.

'*Hetti?* Yes, I know who Hetti is. I just don't understand why she would have mentioned me to you.'

She and Hetti had worked together for a couple of years back at Allport Infirmary's A&E. They'd even been friends. Well, as close to being friends as two rather guarded individuals could be. Probably that was one of their shared traits, which had drawn them to each other.

'She mentioned that you were caught on the horns of a dilemma—not wanting a date for the charity gala on one side and risking being hit on all night if you're without a date on the other. Apparently you've swiftly shut down any man who has asked you.'

Nothing about Nell, then. That was good. The last thing she wanted was people gossiping about her having been a teenage mum, or privately questioning whether she was *really* up to the job of being an air ambulance doctor. It was such a demanding, limited environment, and lives literally depended on her and her two paramedics.

No one else. Just the three of them. Not like in the A&E, where she'd been a doctor up until now, where she could call on a colleague for a consult if she needed to.

So she was still new to the air ambulance team—still in her probationary period. Her employers might have liked her CV and her references, and the way she'd come across in her many interviews, but they didn't know the first thing about her. Mainly because she kept her private life just that. Utterly private.

If they'd known the truth about her would they still have hired her? Would she have been good enough for them? Or even *enough*?

A jolt of something that felt altogether too much like insecurity bolted through Effie before she could stop it. Before she could shove it back into the distant shadows of her brain where it belonged.

The only person who had never made her feel she had something to prove was Eleanor. The one woman who had seen through Effie's tough, angry exterior to the frightened, lonely kid beneath. The woman who had loved her so much that she'd been willing to fight Effie's sorry excuse for a mum and to adopt her. The woman who had seen Effie's potential and encouraged her to really *do* something with her life—starting by going to university. And not just any university, either.

But Eleanor had been gone from her life for so many years now that it was getting harder and harder for Effie to remember how it had felt to have someone to lean on.

It would hardly have been surprising if her bosses and colleagues had panicked about hiring a single mum with a young daughter. If Nell was ill she couldn't just call in sick herself, like other parents. There was no one to cover her. Her team depended on her being there every single time she was supposed to be. On never being distracted.

Including right now.

Effie jutted out her chin and met his gaze. 'And so you stepped up to save me from myself? How chivalrous.'

Her tone was a little tighter, a little sharper than she might have preferred, but that was better than giving in to this absurd heat trapped low in her belly. The kind which threatened to melt a girl from the inside out.

Surely she was past all that nonsense? Hadn't having a baby at eighteen taught her that much, at least?

'You could call it chivalrous. Or you could call it selfish. I'd prefer the term *mutually beneficial.*'

'Really?' Even as she asked, she knew it was a bad sign that it made a difference to her. Made her a little bit too eager for an excuse to break her usual no dating code. 'So what do I gain from it?'

'Hetti mentioned you were too career-focussed to have time to date, and that your move here has invited attention. Fresh blood and all that. We both know that attending this function alone would be tantamount to inviting people to hit on you all night. Going with me should make anyone else leave you alone.'

She could point out that it sounded arrogant for him to say that other men would naturally back away if Tak was her date. The problem was she could imagine that was exactly what would happen.

'Fine. So what about you? Is this your way of ensuring no-strings sex for the night? Because I have to say it's a pretty pathetic way of—'

'No sex,' he cut in definitively.

'Sorry?'

'If I want sex I can get sex. The point is that I don't.'

'A single man in his thirties who doesn't want sex?' Incredibly she found herself raising an eyebrow at him as though she was actually...*flirting*?

'I don't want sex with *you*,' he corrected.

How was it possible to feel suddenly deflated when she didn't want complications herself?

'Oh. Right.' She sounded so stiff, so wooden. 'Well, good. Glad that's cleared up.'

He raked his hand through his hair and she

found the unexpectedly boyish gesture all the more disarming.

'I didn't mean it to sound that way.' Clearly this was as close as she was going to get to an apology. 'My point is that I want a date as a buffer. I don't want complications from it. My extended family have it in their collective heads that if I'm not going to find a wife for myself then they need to find one for me. A date will buy me some time.'

There was no reason for her chest to constrict the way it did at that moment. No reason at all.

'Couldn't you just tell them *no*?'

'I could…' He shrugged, as though it didn't matter to him one way or another. 'I have. Many times. But that doesn't stop them from trying and pushing. I was just about to offend every single one of them by making it unequivocally clear that I'm not interested. However, it's been pointed out to me that there is another way to handle it. A softer way.'

'By Hetti, by chance?'

'Indeed.' Tak flashed another of those wicked smiles which seemed to liquefy her insides within seconds. 'She also pointed out that if I do that they'll turn their focus on her. And no doubt redouble their efforts in revenge.'

Curious.

Hetti had alluded to the fact that her big brother was always looking out for her but, given

Tak's formidable reputation, Effie hadn't really bought it.

'And so you're trying to project a softer Tak Basu? Now, *there's* a curious notion.'

The words were out before she could swallow them. Revealing far more than she might have wanted him to know. Effie could have kicked herself.

'Is it, indeed?'

His eyebrows lifted, his incorrigible expression stealing her breath from her lungs. God, he was magnificent. It should be illegal.

She forced herself to straighten her spine, make her tone just that bit choppier. 'Although conning your extended family is one thing, but conning your mother rather than simply telling her the truth—'

'You don't know what you're talking about.' His low, deep voice, every word uttered with a razor-sharp edge, cut her instantly. 'Consequently, I suggest you don't even try.'

Despite the words he'd used, it would clearly be a mistake to actually believe it had been merely a suggestion.

Effie swallowed. Hard.

Silence enveloped them, and she found herself unable to move. Awkward in her own skin.

His expression softened. 'I shouldn't have spoken to you that way,' he said, and abruptly Effie realised this was Tak apologising to her. 'I'm just…a little protective of my family.'

It was such a familiar pain that it shouldn't hurt her as much as it did. Her throat felt too tight, but somehow she managed to reply. 'That's… admirable.'

What would she have given, growing up, to have had a family who were protective of each other. Even one of her foster families. But instead…

She shuddered at the memories. An endless merry-go-round of girls' homes and foster families, all of whom had either looked at her as though she should be grateful to them for even knowing her name, or else had resented the fact that she wasn't an adorable baby they could cuddle. Or worse. But she didn't like to remember the nights she'd spent sleeping rough on park benches because it had been safer than any given foster home.

There had been a couple of nice families. She could remember both of them with such clarity. They had wanted to adopt her and she'd prayed that they would, even though she'd long since had any sense of faith knocked out of her. But on both occasions her biological mother had somehow— shockingly—managed to convince the authorities that she had gone clean, and they had been compelled to return Effie to her.

Of course it had never lasted.

'I suppose you might call it admirable...' Tak's voice mercifully broke into her thoughts. 'Either way, it seems we both have our reasons for wanting a buffer.'

'I can handle myself.' She narrowed her eyes at him, irked to concede that he might actually have a point.

'I'm suggesting that you don't *have* to. That our attending the ball together could make it a smoother night all around.'

'Right...' she conceded slowly, without knowing why.

'So, do we have a deal?'

There were a hundred reasons why she should say no. Thirteen of them even had the same four letters. Nell. But suddenly all Effie could think of were all the reasons—as flimsy and as spurious as she knew them to be—why she might say yes.

'My car is in the garage right now, so it would save me having to drive myself...'

She couldn't believe she'd said it aloud. It didn't even sound believable. What on earth had made her think it was better to say that than admit her car was such a clapped-out old mess she didn't want people seeing her in it in case they asked too many questions?

It had been bad enough convincing her new colleagues that she kept it because it had sentimental value, rather than tell the truth about the fact that she'd been going to change it, but Nell's new school had offered a last-minute place on a ski trip they'd been planning for twelve months and, given the lateness, she'd needed to make full payment of a sum which had made her eyes water.

She knew what people's expectation of a doctor's salary was—and why they couldn't equate her career with her always-tight finances. Even those who know about her daughter.

However much the news made an issue of student debt, and the tens of thousands that medical students especially could incur, it was easy for outsiders to forget that such debt incurred heavy interest every year. Even many of her colleagues had had family to support them financially, at least to some degree.

But none of them had also been raising a daughter at the same time.

Effie still shuddered when she thought of how she'd had to beg and plead—and sometimes gloss a little over the truth—in order to secure every available student and bank loan out there. She could have chosen a different career, of course, but she'd had something to prove. Both to herself and in memory of the one woman who had ever believed in her.

Even when she'd qualified, every penny of her salary had been swallowed up, not just by basic living costs, but by the additional costs that a child had incurred. Food, children's clothes which never seemed to fit for more than a year, but especially the crippling childcare costs, Especially for a junior doctor working long shifts, night shifts, and even sometimes ninety-plus hour weeks.

True, nowadays her career was more established and she was a lot more financially stable, but even now she couldn't break the habit of putting her daughter first. Maybe it was because she needed to give Nell the opportunities she herself had never had, or perhaps it was guilt at having had to work so hard for all those years.

Either way, it was why her clever, beautiful, funny daughter was at the most prestigious private school in the area, to the tune of several tens of thousands a year—even without the additional ski trips, French exchanges, and Summer Activities program—whilst she herself kept her old car for just one year longer.

Not that she would ever confess to someone a single word of any of that to someone like Tak.

Still, his expression flickered slightly and Effie couldn't be sure what he was thinking. She had a feeling he was laughing at her and she gave herself a mental kick. And then she kicked herself again for even caring what he thought about her.

Good job she was immune to cocky, arrogant, too-handsome-for-their-own-good playboys.

Although the way her traitorous heart was reacting to him was galling. This never happened to her. *Never.* She had never gossiped with colleagues about the latest developments in an eligible guy's sex-life. Or lusted after men around the water cooler. Or gone out to clubs and picked up guys.

That didn't mean she hadn't lusted after the odd guy on TV, or in a magazine. Though never in person—not like this. At least not since Nell's father, as gargantuan a mistake as *he* had been. Not that she would ever give Nell up for a second. But he had been an idiot boy whom she'd lusted after but never loved. Had barely even known—not really. He'd had no hopes, no dreams. He'd relied on his good looks and he certainly hadn't wanted to *achieve* anything. He'd laughed at her dreams of going to university to study medicine. Told her to get real. That places like that didn't take kids like them.

They'd dated—if it could even be called that—for a handful of months. And even that had been because a lethal cocktail of grief and lust, had given her the desire to get one thing to make her forget the other, if only for one night.

Eleanor's shocking death had rocked her more than all those awful years in and out of foster homes, or care homes when her mother had been deemed 'too unfit' to care for her. The fact that something as ugly and banal as a drunk driver could have snuffed out such a warm, glorious light, in the blink of an eye, made it that much worse.

In a matter of hours Effie had gone from being

on the brink of being adopted, and finally having a loving family in the form of Eleanor, to having absolutely no one. No one but him. And she'd let herself believe that he could ease her loneliness.

But when she told him she'd fallen pregnant he'd wanted nothing to do with her, and she'd never felt more abandoned. That had been the moment she'd vowed she would never again let anyone into her personal life, never let a guy know she was attracted to them.

Immune, she reminded herself now, crossly.

Tearing her eyes away from the approaching figure, Effie checked her watch. 'I have to get back to the heli.'

'No one's stopping you.' Tak twisted his mouth into something which was too amused to be a smile. 'You're the one who has prolonged things, preferring this verbal sparring to answering a simple question.'

It was as though he could read her thoughts. As though he knew that a part of her was aching to say *yes.*

Effie drew herself up as tall as she could. 'Is that right?' she managed primly. 'Then allow me to be clear. My answer, Dr Basu, is *no.* No, I do *not* want to accompany you to the hospital charity ball as your date. Fake or otherwise.'

So why was every fibre of her screaming at her that this was the wrong answer?

'I see.' His lips twitched. 'Thank you for letting me know.'

Before she could ruin the moment, Effie filed away her notes and marched out through the Resus doors. It took her a moment to realise that she wasn't alone.

Spinning around, she confronted him. 'Why are you following me?'

'Apologies if it's spoiling the dramatic effect of your exit.' Tak didn't look remotely apologetic. 'I'm heading home. My car is in the car park next to the helipad.'

He had to be kidding?

She hesitated, unsure what to do next. It was a two-hundred-metre stretch from here to there. If she marched off ahead of him he might think she was employing one of those flirtatious tactics of making him look at her backside. But the alternative was walking together in an awkward silence.

There was no reason for that to hold the slightest amount of appeal, she berated herself silently. Perhaps it would be easier if she pretended she'd forgotten something inside the hospital and headed back inside for a moment? Yes, that might be best.

Turning around, Effie took a step towards the hospital doors just as one of her more dogged suitors—who had so far asked her out three times and showed no signs of getting the message—walked out.

A smarmy smile slid over his features and she panicked. A little bit of pursuit might be considered flattering, but the problem with this particular guy was that he truly deemed himself too good a catch for any woman in their right mind to reject him. It seemed the more she turned him down, the more he took it as a challenge that she wanted to be pursued harder.

She could report him, of course, but she needed the money and not the hassle.

Her brain spun on its wheels. For the second time in as many moments she turned to Tak, ignoring the little voice inside her head which was doing the most inappropriate celebratory jig all on its own.

'So, what time did you say you'd collect me for the hospital ball?'

She could see it instantly. His eyes flicking from her to her would-be admirer, then back again. Sizing up the situation in an instant. Then there was that wicked gleam in his eye which had her heart beating faster as she wondered whether or not he was about to land her in it.

For a long moment, they stared at each other. Amusement danced across his rich brown eyes, whilst she could only imagine the desperate plea in her own. Finally, Tak spoke.

'Shall we say seven-thirty?'

'Seven-thirty.' She bobbed her head—a little too much like the nodding dog in the back of one of her foster family's cars for her own liking. 'I'm looking forward to it.'

She should hate it that a traitorous part of her actually was.

CHAPTER THREE

'YOU DIDN'T HAVE to wait down here.'

Tak frowned as he sauntered into her lobby like some kind of Hollywood action hero. Sleek and burnished and sheer masculine magnificence—a stark contrast to the shabby, grubby, in-need-of-repair surroundings.

Effie felt her heartbeat actually hang for a moment, before galloping wildly back into life as an unexpected, unwanted tingle coursed over her skin. It was a momentary reprieve from the anxiety which had flushed her body ever since her daughter had dropped the mother of all bombshells on her, barely a few minutes ago. Just as she'd been about to walk out of the door.

If it hadn't been for the knowledge that Tak would come up to the flat if she wasn't in the lobby to stop him, she might have dropped everything and spent the entire night talking to—or rather yelling at—her daughter about her monumentally stupid lapse in judgement.

In some ways this night with Tak was a silver lining. It would give her space and a chance to calm down. If she blurted out to her daughter all the things that were racing around her head at this moment in time, then she might easily ruin their relationship for a long, long time to come.

Still, Effie told herself darkly that her reaction to Tak was simply due to the rush of cold night air accompanying his entrance.

She knew it wasn't true.

So much for her efforts these past couple of days in telling herself that she had a handle on the situation. That her initial reaction to Tak had simply been a result of being caught off-guard. That now she'd had exposure to him she would be able to build up her resistance.

How on earth had she ever agreed to this?

'I would have come to your door,' he continued pointedly.

Effie thought of Nell, several storeys above them, and was pretty sure her daughter could sense her fury from all the way up there in the flat. And that was without the additional consideration of old Mrs Appleby from next door, who was babysitting Nell and never let the fact that she was practically deaf prevent her from sniffing out even a whiff of gossip. Seeing Tak Basu would be her scoop of the year. Of the decade, even.

'It's fine.' She shook her head and forced a smile. 'It isn't a proper date, remember?'

For the next few hours she would welcome the distraction. It would do her and Nell good to have the evening apart. Time to think.

'I'm glad to see that *you* do.' His voice sounded different from how she remembered. As if he was distracted. 'Although I should say you look stunning.'

Heat flooded her cheeks—and something else that she didn't care to identify. She pretended it was merely concern that people might recognise her dress for the cheap, off-the-sale-rack, several-seasons-old gown that it was.

'Thank you.'

It didn't seem to matter how many times she told herself that he didn't mean anything by it, that it was just something any date would say—fake or otherwise. Her body didn't seem in the least bit interested in listening to such reason.

'Your hair is…stunning.'

She didn't know how she managed to stop her hands from lifting automatically to touch her head. It had taken her hours to get her hair like this—she would say she was hopelessly out of practice, but she wasn't sure she'd ever been *in* practice—and she was pleased with the results. Thick, glossy, soft curls. It was the most glamorous she'd felt in a long time.

It was only fitting that she should spoil it all by saying something ridiculously prosaic and work-related. 'Did you know there's a study showing that natural redheads often need around twenty percent more anaesthetic than people with other hair colours to reach the same levels of sedation?'

'There have been several studies,' he confirmed gravely, but she couldn't shake the impression that he was concealing his amusement. 'They appear to confirm redheads as a distinct phenotype linked to anaesthetic requirement.'

Of course he knew. He was a neurosurgeon, after all. Well, that was her bank of small talk exhausted. Not that it seemed to matter when her brain froze as he stepped up to her and offered his arm.

For one brief moment the sight of Tak—so mouth-wateringly handsome in a bespoke tuxedo, the cut of which somehow achieved the impossible by allowing his already well-built body to look all the more powerful and dangerous— made her wonder what it would be like to go on a *real* date with someone like him.

She might have said made her *yearn*, had she not already known that was impossible. She hadn't yearned in over thirteen years. She'd learned that bitter lesson—although she would never change her precious daughter for anything in the world.

Effie clicked her tongue impatiently—more at herself than the man standing in front of her. 'Right, shall we go and get this over with?'

'A woman after my own heart,' he said, and his mouth twisted into something which looked more like the baring of teeth than an actual smile.

And then he stepped closer, his hand to the small of her back to guide her, and it was all Effie could do not to shiver at the delicious contact. She could put it down to nerves, and the fact that this was the first time she'd been out in two years—ever since the last hospital gala she'd been compelled to attend and had hated every moment—but she suspected that wasn't the true root of it.

'There's no reason to feel nervous—' He stopped abruptly. 'Did you know we'd met before when we talked the other day?'

She twisted her head to look at him, surprised that he remembered her. 'Yes, actually. I brought one of the first casualties I ever attended with the air ambulance to your hospital. You were the neurology consultant. Left-sided temporal parietal hematoma.'

'Douglas Jacobs.'

'You remember his name? I'm impressed.'

'I remember,' Tak confirmed.

She couldn't have said what it was about his tone, but in that instant he made her believe that he remembered *all* his patients. That they weren't just bodies to him. They were people.

It took her aback. Worse. It made him all the more fascinating.

'You're the one who diagnosed the expressive aphasia?' Tak asked.

It had been in the notes, but she knew he was testing her. Because it mattered to him. It was a heady thought.

'I did.' It was all she could to sound casual. As

though her body *wasn't* beginning to fizz deliriously at Tak's interest.

'He wasn't talking much and his vitals were stable. You did well to spot it. It was very subtle on presentation.'

His compliment *didn't* send a tingle rushing along her spine. Not at all.

'It worsened over time?' she asked.

'Very quickly, I'm afraid.' Tak nodded. 'CT revealed a depressed skull fracture and an underlying subdural bleed, so we took him straight into an OR. When he awoke the aphasia was still present, but reduced.'

'So he's in rehab?' She squeezed her eyes shut, remembering how sweet the guy had been, and how close he and his worried wife had seemed.

'He is,' Tak confirmed. 'He's doing well, and he has a good support network, so with any luck he should be fine.'

'That's good.' She smiled, more to herself than at Tak.

It occurred to her that he'd been distracting her. Telling her a story—a work-related story—which he'd known would make her feel less tense, more at ease.

She should be angry that he'd played her, but instead she just felt grateful to him.

Allowing Tak to guide her to a large, chauffeur-driven limousine, she slid inside, trying not to marvel at the bespoke rich plaid wool and leather seats. And then he was climbing in gracefully beside her, closing the door, and the entire back seat seemed to shrink until she was aware of nothing but how very close his body was to hers.

Now it was just the two of them together, in such a confined space, it was impossible for her to keep up the pretence. To keep telling herself that his voice *didn't* swirl inside her like a fog which refused to clear, that his eyes *didn't* look right into her soul as though they could read every last dark secret in there, that his touch *didn't* send electricity coursing through her veins only to conclude in a shower of sparks as breathtaking as the best fireworks display.

The realisation thrilled and terrorised her in equal measure.

'You shouldn't be embarrassed about where you live, you know.'

It took a moment for her to focus, and then another for shame and guilt to steal through her. 'I'm not,' she said, and lifted her chin a little higher.

'Then why did you insist on meeting me in the lobby instead of letting me pick you up from your apartment?'

'I just... It wasn't about being embarrassed.' Not entirely true, but close enough.

'Then what *was* it about?'

There was no justification at all for her wanting to tell him the truth. Effie had spent her whole life shutting people out—as soon as she'd learned it was either that or *be* shut out. It shouldn't be difficult to tell Tak to mind his own business.

Yet there was a quality about him which reminded her of the one woman who had cared for her, helped her so long ago. She couldn't explain it, nor shake it. It was bizarre. This wasn't even a proper date, and the fact that she kept finding that detail so difficult to remember was concerning in itself.

'It wasn't about where I live, although I know it's no penthouse. It was more about keeping the two parts of my life separate. My private life and my professional one.'

'Does it matter that much?'

Was she guarding her personal details because they were none of his business? The way she would keep any other one of her colleagues at bay? Or was there a part of her that wished she could be—just for one night—the kind of carefree single woman that a man like Tak might actually *want* to date? And not just pretend.

Ridiculous.

Guilt speared her. She *wasn't* that kind of woman. She had barely been that kind of girl. Her carefree single days had ended the moment she'd found out that she was going to become a teenage mum. And there had been absolutely no one in the world to support her.

For the last thirteen years it had been just her and Nell. Together. She was ashamed that a part of her should want to pretend otherwise, even for a few hours.

'Yes, it does matter.' She nodded. *It was now or never.* 'To me. And to my daughter.'

Silence dropped between them like the thick, heavy curtain on a stage, separating the players from the audience. Her from Tak. What on earth had possessed her to say anything? Was it simply because Tak reminded her of a woman who was long gone?

'You have a daughter?'

His voice was even, just as before. Perhaps the silence had only been in her own head.

'Nell. Short for Eleanor. She's thirteen.'

'Thirteen? You must have been…'

'Just turned eighteen.' She didn't mean to sound so snappy, but she couldn't stop herself. 'Yeah, you don't have to do the maths. I've lived it. Now you know why I don't date. Why I *won't* date.'

Whatever she'd been expecting him to say, it wasn't the words which came next. Or the soft, almost melancholy tone.

'Difficult age, thirteen. I imagine she hasn't taken kindly to the move?'

She floundered. 'Um…no. Not really.'

'She's acting out?'

It was less of a question, more of a statement. As though he knew. And there was something else, too. Effie couldn't quite pinpoint what it was, but if she'd had to hazard a guess she might have thought that he didn't *like* the fact that he knew. That he felt it was a connection between them which he didn't want to feel.

Hadn't Hetti once told her that Tak had spent much of his childhood taking care of his younger siblings—not just the usual big-brother-as-play-ground-protector stuff, but all the tasks that a parent would ordinarily do? If that was true then it had to be hard for him to shake that responsibility, even now they were all grown up.

It was certainly hard for herself, trying to let go of the past. Trying not to let it cloud the way she dealt with Nell. Trying not to let her own life experiences turn her into an over-protective mother. But maybe she was just imagining it. Either way, it was all she could do not to nod in agreement and wonder…

'What makes you say that?' she asked.

'Because you were agitated when I met you in the lobby. Like you'd had a run-in with someone. I assumed it was the teenage lads I saw hanging around outside.'

'Those lads are fine. And the place isn't that bad. It's a desirable city-centre location. Besides, it's the closest thing I could find to Nell's new school on such short notice.'

'Desirable is a matter of opinion,' he disputed. 'So the run-in was with someone else? I'm thinking it was with your daughter. Nell. Want to talk about it?'

'Nope.' But she couldn't fault him for being astute. It was impressive, really.

'It might help.'

She opened her mouth, then snapped it shut again. Surely she shouldn't be discussing this with him, an almost stranger? Effie wanted to shut the conversation down, but found that she couldn't. There was something about Tak, about those broad shoulders, which suddenly made her think how nice it would be to get another perspective and some adult support.

She did, however, find herself tugging on a stray thread from her clutch bag. A habit she'd formed decades ago, when she was anxious and unhappy. Or feeling cornered.

'I don't see why I would talk about it,' she managed stiffly.

'Because everyone needs to talk sometimes.'

She might have believed him if she hadn't caught the flash of irritation in his expression. However fleeting it had been.

Being a foster kid had made her sensitive— some might argue *over*-sensitive—to when people were asking questions out of a sense of obligation rather than any actual desire to hear the answer.

What she didn't understand was why she wasn't consequently shutting the conversation down with her usual practised efficiency. Why any part of her was actually considering opening up to Tak Basu, of all people. It was madness.

'Who says I don't already have someone to talk to?' She twisted her mouth before catching herself. 'If I need to, that is.'

'Maybe you do.' He shrugged. 'But I think you're too pent-up...too defensive. As though you're trying to deal with too much all by yourself. A teenage girl comes complete with a wealth of complications. Trust me—I know.'

For a moment his eyes met hers, deep brown and filled with understanding, as if they were stealing her very soul. And it hurt simply to breathe.

Effie didn't understand what was happening. Not inside this car, and certainly not inside *her*. She had the oddest sense of...*connection*. As if something was binding them and she didn't understand what it was.

Then the vehicle stopped, and she realised they had arrived at the gala. Plastering a bright smile on her lips, she tore her gaze away and injected an upbeat note into her voice. 'We're here—shall we go in?'

He didn't answer straight away, and the moment stretched out tautly between them until he finally inclined his head. 'As you wish.'

And as the driver opened their doors to let them out Effie told herself that she was relieved.

CHAPTER FOUR

TAK WAS GRATEFUL to be released from that endless icy blue gaze of hers. The one which was flecked with shards of gold. The one which shot right through him to the deepest caverns of his chest, expanding and shattering all that it touched.

At least he told himself that he was grateful. He was pretty sure that what he actually felt was a damn sight closer to disappointed. Yet that made no sense at all.

Moving around the vehicle to walk Effie up the steps and into the imposing, architecturally spectacular old building, he couldn't help himself placing his hand at the small of her back, and the jolt of awareness at the contact both took him by surprise and, simultaneously, did not.

It was a long, long time since any woman had sneaked under his skin the way this woman had. If ever. It was rather extraordinary. It made a part of him want to whisk her away from here, from these people and the crowds, and take her somewhere quiet where he might actually be able to talk to her. One on one.

A preposterous notion.

The problem was that he'd been entirely floored by her the moment he'd walked into that grotty lobby and seen her standing there, so startlingly beautiful, so elegant, looking so wholly incongruous to her surroundings.

He'd wanted to pick her up and carry her out of there, if only so that her feet didn't have to tread a single step on that filthy stone floor. If there had been a puddle he might even have thrown down his cloak, or at least his jacket.

Then again, if he'd picked her up, taken her in his arms, he might have been in even more trouble than he was in now. Because if simply *looking* at that tantalising body was having such an effect on him, then what might touching it actually do?

That orange flight suit hadn't even hinted at the glorious figure now poured into a dress which looked as though it had been hand-crafted just for Effie. All soft, lush, feminine curves, deliciously naughty, which drew the eye and yet had the brain filling in the gaps for all the other senses.

God, how he wanted to see what that body was like beneath those clothes. Feel it pressed against his. Lick every last inch of it…

Tak came back to his senses with a rude crash. What was he thinking? This wasn't even a real date—it certainly wasn't going to end up like *that*. Wasn't that the whole point of them coming here together? To avoid such complications?

Whatever was going on here wasn't in the script. It hadn't been in the plan. The sooner he got tonight over with and took this bewitching woman back home, the better. In fact he should start by finding Hetti—after all, wasn't she the one who had asked him to bring Effie here?

So why, instead, did he find himself guiding her inside? Find his hand moving from a light touch on her back to something arguably more possessive in sliding around to her waist to draw her in closer as several male colleagues made no attempt to conceal their envy? And why did a sense of triumph pound through him when Effie seemed to lean in to him that little bit closer, as if seeking his protection?

Unexpectedly, a couple of women caught his arm on the way in, flirting with him without a single glance at the woman who had come in on his arm, and Effie disengaged herself lightly, discreetly, in order to step ahead.

His head was still stuck back in his earlier conversation with her, and he let her go. It hit him several seconds later, when it felt altogether too much like a loss. Suddenly Tak found himself quickening his pace just to catch up with her.

'What are you doing?'

She blinked, as though she wasn't quite sure of herself. 'Giving you space.'

Something moved through him. Something hot and frustrated. Like temper, only not quite. 'Do I need to remind you that the whole idea of us coming together was to be each other's buffer?'

'I know that.' She tried to sound indignant, but

couldn't disguise the catch in her voice. 'But you didn't seem to want a buffer from those women.'

Was she jealous? He was unreasonably glad.

'I disagree. Giving me space rather defeats the purpose, wouldn't you say?'

She looked at him, and there was something too bright, too electric for comfort in her gaze.

'So we're really doing this?'

'Doing what?'

'Pretending to be a couple?' Her voice faltered. 'Not just arriving together but...*being* together?'

It hadn't been his original intention. *Had it?*

'That's exactly what we're going to do,' he said.

She swallowed, but he could read women well enough to know it wasn't out of any kind of sense of feeling intimidated. She was fighting this attraction just as he was. She *wanted* him.

The knowledge shot through to Tak's very core.

Another group of women appeared without warning. 'Show-time,' he muttered, too quietly for anyone else to hear. 'Let's make it a good one. Can you do that?'

She scowled at him, which did nothing at all to lessen her beauty, then tipped her chin upwards. 'Of course I can,' she declared. 'I can play any game just as well as you can.'

He stamped out the voice in his head telling him he wished it wasn't quite such a game and led her into the crowd.

* * *

It turned out that Effie could indeed play any game as well as he could, Tak was forced to acknowledge several hours later. Perhaps even better.

She had charmed everyone to whom he'd introduced her. More like the bold, confident doctor he'd watched in action than the nervous, self-conscious woman who had been standing in that apartment lobby tonight, shifting her weight awkwardly from one foot to the other.

All evening he'd watched her smile and chat and laugh, so skilful that she had befriended the women whilst simultaneously captivating the men. It was a completely different side to her from the professional, even standoffish, air ambulance doctor he had seen a few days ago. Who cared for her patients but who had no time whatsoever for the flirtations of her eager colleagues.

Now she was gracious and sweet, even coquettish, and as far as anyone was concerned very much *his.* She had leaned into him, her fingertips brushing his arm, her fringe skimming his chin, with that flirty little laugh floating around the two of them had almost bound them, despite the rest of the crowd in the room.

No wonder she had fooled the other guests perfectly, even better than he could have imagined she would. Because at times she had nearly fooled him. He, Tak Basu, had found himself caught up in the moment, caught up in *her*, scowling at any other man who might get a bit too close, whose hand might linger on Effie's that fraction too long. As if he was feeling jealous. Possessive. When the entire world knew that wasn't him.

He should move away. Re-establish a few boundaries. Instead he found himself bending down until his mouth was by her ear, far closer than it had any need to be. 'There's still a few minutes on the silent auction,' he murmured, revelling in the way her skin instantly goosebumped. 'Shall we take a punt together?'

Obediently she moved with him in one single direction-change. 'I thought you'd already made your bids? Quite a few of them, if I recall correctly.'

'I did,' he returned smoothly. 'The Grand Master golf experience is for Rafi, the balloon ride for Hetti and the chocolatier master class for Sasha. Plus I always enjoy a race day. But I didn't bid on anything which might be considered remotely romantic. The Parisian weekend for two, for instance…'

He shouldn't celebrate the way her eyes dilated, nor the way her nostrils gave a tiny flare. And he certainly shouldn't exult in the resultant shallow, squally breaths.

'It's a fake date,' she managed.

'Indeed it is. But no one here knows that. It's been *quite* an impressive performance you've managed this evening…' His voice was far softer than he'd intended, and he watched as she struggled to compose herself.

'I could argue that your performance was even more outstanding.'

'I make a point of ensuring *all* my performances are outstanding.'

'We… I mean, I… That is…you…' Effie stumbled, a delectable crimson blush staining her cheeks.

This reversion to her more prim side was a welcome step away from her flirtatiousness. Why was it that he couldn't get enough of the overly demure, innocent side of Effie?

'I apologise.' He grinned and let her off the hook. 'That was uncalled-for. Now, what about that weekend for two?'

She cleared her throat delicately. Once. Twice. 'Say all of your bids turn out to be the highest?'

'Then I go home a very successful man.'

He couldn't have said what had changed in her expression but he noticed it. Just as he noticed the way she began absently pulling at a loose thread on her clutch.

'That's got to be an obscene amount of money.'

Tak balked at the edge in her voice. His tone when he answered was harsher than he had intended. 'When was the last time you and Nell went abroad?'

'Nell's going skiing in a few weeks.'

He didn't miss the dark shadows dulling her blue eyes, for a moment turning them almost grey.

'And you?'

'Does it matter?'

'Humour me.'

'No.'

'Have you *ever* been abroad?' He had no idea what made him ask the question. It wasn't as though he knew the first thing about this relative stranger.

She chewed on her lip, her discomfort undeniable.

'I was a junior doctor and a single mother with a young kid.'

His voice softened of its own volition. 'I'll take that as a *no.*'

She glowered at him, but still said nothing. And, as with all the little nuggets he'd been pretending he hadn't been filing away all evening, he slotted that new piece of information into his mental picture of Dr Effie Robinson.

The real Effie. Not the one she presented to the world.

'Listen, it's no big deal. It's just for charity.'

'Yes…still—' She stopped abruptly.

The slight tic in her jaw betrayed how tightly her teeth were clenched. As though the more he dismissed it as nothing, the more it riled her.

'Just forget it, Tak.'

And he might have forgotten it. Or he might

have defused the situation with his usual ease. But instead Tak found himself focussing on the hostility of her tone. More than that, *welcoming* it.

Because if she was being judgemental then here, finally, was something which knocked her off the virtual pedestal upon which he couldn't even remember putting her. He could shake off this inexplicable attraction which snaked constantly between them.

Tonight was about making other people wonder about him and Effie and if they were in a relationship. It wasn't about making *himself* wonder what it would be like to be in a relationship with the woman. It made no sense.

He barely contained a *harrumph* of displeasure. Even if a part of him *was* attracted to her, there was still no way he was going to go there. She had a daughter. Responsibilities. Something told him that she wasn't the kind of woman to be interested in a one-night stand. By contrast, he'd lost his entire childhood by taking responsibility for his siblings and it had put him off marriage and children for life. So the last thing he needed was to get involved with a woman who came complete with a ready-made family.

Which begged the question as to why he was intrigued by the woman standing so straight-backed in front of him at this instant. He used it to prod Effie and rile her all the more. 'You resent me doing it because the more obscene the amount of money I spend, the more it draws attention to us.'

'No, it isn't… Well, it doesn't…' She drew in a deep breath. 'Like I said, forget it.'

'Isn't that why you agreed to this charade? Because you knew dating…?'

'*Fake* dating,' she interjected.

Her teeth were gritted so tightly he was sure her jaw had to be in pain. So what made him flash his most wolfish smile?

'All right.' He inclined his head as if amused, though they both heard the sharp edge to his words. 'You knew that by fake dating someone as high-profile as me that word would get around the hospital faster than a superbug.'

'Yes, but—'

'No buts.' He cut her off. 'Part of my high-profile status is down to my wealth. But you already knew that—so why is it suddenly so distasteful to you?'

'It isn't.'

She pursed her lips and he didn't doubt that she was holding back, biting down the words she desperately wanted to say. He couldn't have said why that got to him the way that it did.

And then another thought struck him. One which he knew instantly wasn't true, even though he couldn't have said *how* he knew that. But he couldn't stop himself from voicing it all the same.

'Or perhaps that was what you *wanted* me to think?'

She stopped. Blinked at him. Leaving Tak with the oddest sensation that he was skating over the thinnest sliver of sparkling blue ice: ice that could crack at any second, letting him plunge into dark, fatal, sub-zero depths.

'Say that again?' Even her voice crackled icily.

'Is that what you *want* me to think, Effie? That my money repels you? You must know how many women are attracted to the lifestyle I could offer them. Just as you've probably heard how little women like that appeal to me. Did you think you could reel me in if you pretended to abhor the material side of things?'

'What? *No!*' She managed to look angry, insulted and hurt all at once. 'Is that what you truly believe?'

No. 'It's possible.'

'It's ludicrous.' She sniffed, somewhat inelegantly. 'Do I need to remind you that this whole thing was *your* idea. Not mine.'

'Hetti's.'

'Pardon?'

'It was Hetti's idea,' he repeated coolly, calmly, though he had no idea how he managed to be either. 'Maybe *you* just saw a way to get to my money.'

It wasn't supposed to be going this way. He wasn't meant to be this affected by Effie. He felt

like the kind of floundering, out-of-his-depth adolescent he'd never actually been. It was ludicrous.

Effie, meanwhile, sucked in a breath, her face
pinched and white. Yet, to her credit, she held
herself straight and tall. The epitome of dignity.

'Whilst that may be true, I could also point out
that you may be making your own money *now*,
but much of what you have comes from having
a famous gynaecologist for a father and the *in*famous Basu wealth.'

Anger bubbled through him, and even that, too,
was welcoming in its own way. He'd learned to
contain his emotions from such a young age, trying to keep his sisters and brother in check and
getting along, that he found it hard to do anything
else as he grew up, bottling things up too often.

What *was* it about Effie that got under his skin
in a way that no one and nothing else had been
able to do for so many years?

He opened his mouth to respond, but Effie beat
him to it.

'And, for the record, I didn't want to do this
but *you* pursued me.'

'I was under the illusion that you were shy, re-
tiring and aloof—not some kind of siren capable
of charming every man she meets,' he bit out.

*Hell's teeth, what was that? He sounded al-
most...possessive. Jealous.*

He was only grateful that Effie was barrelling
on, clearly oblivious.

'Well, then, may I say that *I* was equally duped. The man your sister described to me was a focussed genius doctor and a kind and dedicated brother. *You*, however, are acting like a spoilt brat.'

God, but she was truly stunning. Flame-haired and flame-tongued, her arctic blue gaze as lethal as a pick-axe stabbing shards of ice off a gloriously frozen waterfall.

'I'm sorry.'

The apology came out of nowhere. Apparently to both of them. But suddenly it actually mattered to him how this evening went.

She eyed him warily. 'You're sorry?'

'I was baiting you,' he conceded flatly. 'I'm sorry.'

'Why? Why were you baiting me, I mean?'

There was no reason at all for him to want to be honest with her. But… 'It was beginning to feel a little too much like a proper date.' He shrugged. 'I didn't want there to be…mixed signals. Ridiculous, I know.'

She hesitated before muttering a reply. 'Not entirely ridiculous.'

He liked the flush which crept up her neck. Perhaps a little bit too much. And then, as though he couldn't help himself, he thought of the fact that she had been eighteen when she had a baby. That she had somehow put herself through medical school. It was impossible not to admire the woman.

'I also could have been a little more thought-ful with regard to money. A little more sensitive. It can't have been easy to raise your daughter alone, at that age, and still work towards becoming a doctor.'

He didn't remember moving towards her but suddenly she was right there, and his hand was covering hers, stilling her movements and stopping her from worrying at that loose thread any further.

'Well,' she whispered softly, 'that's my issue to deal with, not yours. And not anyone else's.'

There was something so...*lost* in her expression that he didn't even think about it—didn't even consider how much of his own private past he might be giving away—he simply said the one thing that he wished someone had said to *him* when he'd been eighteen and trying to deal with a bull-headed thirteen-year-old Hetti. Despite everything else, Tak found himself reaching for that connection between them.

'You've done well, Effie. Give yourself a break.'

'I do,' she lied.

His gaze said everything. 'Not enough. I saw how agitated you were when I picked you up from your building. I... I have sisters. I know how hard it is to keep a wilful teenage girl from going off the rails, and I can only imagine what grief your daughter gave you tonight for coming out with me. But that's just part of growing up. And so what if you don't have a lot of money? You've obviously given your daughter love and guidance—and, frankly, one hell of a role model. She'll come back to you at some point.'

Then, because her eyes looked glassy and she seemed as though she was desperately fighting to hold it together, and he knew if he hugged her it might look too obvious that he was comforting her, Tak ushered her quickly back into the main hall and swung her out onto the dance floor before she had time to pull away.

'I don't dance,' she said, panicked.

'All you have to do is follow my lead. Come here.' He cut her off gruffly, drawing her to him and letting her body settle against his, feeling her stiffen, and resist, and then ultimately crumple slightly against him as she realised there would be no release.

He didn't want to analyse what it was that had made him do it. What compunction had caused him to pull her onto the dance floor just so that he could hold her body to his. Where he'd imagined her being all evening.

And, as she pressed her head so tightly against his chest that he wondered if she could hear his heart thumping, Tak couldn't help feeling that this fleeting lowering of her defences was something of a bittersweet victory.

CHAPTER FIVE

EFFIE WAS STARTLED, but then a sense of calm seemed to flow into her. She lifted her gaze to meet his. Those rich mahogany eyes saw so deeply into her she was half afraid he might be able to read her entire past.

First he'd baited her, then he'd argued. And she'd been only too happy to play along, because she'd felt, and resented, the connection that they had. The electric spark. He wasn't the only one to think it felt more like a real date than a fake one. Worse, she couldn't bring herself to lament the fact. As though she wanted something...*more* with him.

'How?' she whispered, barely even hearing her own voice. 'How would you know she'll come back to me?'

'Hetti wasn't the easiest thirteen-year-old. Or fourteen or fifteen-year-old, for that matter. I remember my grandmother used to say, *Oh, to love a child and yet simultaneously want to strangle them.*'

Effie shook her head, not wanting to read too much into this magical insight into the infamously private Tak Basu's life 'You have a whole family. It isn't the same.'

'My father was working...' Something flashed

across his face too fast for her to identify it. 'Mama was…going through her own thing. So I stepped up.'

Why couldn't she shake the impression that there was more to it? Then again, did it matter? Maybe it was the wine making her feel tired, or maybe it was Tak's demeanour, so capable, so authoritative, so *there*, which made her want to stop having to be the strong one—if only for a night— and let someone else bear the weight.

'Nell shoplifted today,' she announced, before she could think better of it.

Because he had been right when he'd said he thought she had no one to talk to, and because he was offering to be that someone, and because it wasn't a real date so why not take him up on it? Not because there was something about him which made her feel some kind of bond. That would be nonsensical.

'You know this how…?'

'She told me. Just before I walked out to come and meet you.'

'Ah.'

'Maybe I should have stayed.' She lifted her shoulders, exhaling deeply. 'Another night I probably would have done. But I just felt so drained, and so angry I was afraid of losing my temper, and I figured the space might do us both good.'

'Wise choice,' he muttered, his gaze never leaving hers, his fingers stroking her hand. As if he might actually...*care.*

It was laughable, of course. He barely knew her, let alone cared about her. Yet it was the closest thing she'd had to caring in a long, long time and, as exhausted as she was, the idea of someone else sharing the burden—if only for a few hours—was altogether too tempting.

'But you know it's a good thing that she told you, don't you? She clearly isn't happy about it, and she knows it's wrong.'

'Of *course* she knows it's wrong,' Effie spluttered. 'I haven't brought her up to think it's acceptable.'

'Relax. No one is questioning your parenting skills. I'm just saying she wanted to tell you, so she wants your help. Even if she doesn't know how to ask for it directly.'

'She knows she can come to me any time.' Effie shook her head. 'With anything.'

'She always has in the past?'

Snapping her head up with a glower, Effie raked her gaze over his face, expecting sarcasm. But she didn't find it. Only empathy.

'Yes.' She couldn't eliminate that last trace of defiance. 'She always has in the past.'

'Because you're friends as well as mother and daughter? And because that was when she was twelve and now she's thirteen? And because that was before you dragged her to a new town and a new school and no doubt ruined her life?'

Despite herself, Effie couldn't help a wry smile. 'All of the above. How did you know?'

'I told you, Hetti wasn't always the super-doc you see now, with her sunny disposition.'

And then he laughed. And everything...*shifted*.

It poured through her like the warm heat of the sun on her skin, permeating right through to her very bones. Making her head spin. She held on tight as he kept dancing, just so that she could keep her balance. But that only pulled her closer to Tak, making things worse.

Or better.

Certainly not clearer. Though she wasn't sure she wanted it to be.

'What did she take?' he asked at length.

'A lipstick.'

'Just the one?'

'That isn't enough?' she breathed. Yet she couldn't help being taken aback by his understanding demeanour.

'You do see that your daughter is still coming to you now, don't you?' he murmured.

It took a moment for her to focus. '*After* the fact,' she managed.

'Which is better than not at all.'

'Not doing it in the first place would be best.'

His wry smile *did* things to her.

'Is this going to be a productive conversation

or just one in which we list comparatives and superlatives?'

'I don't know—do you have any ideas of how to make it more productive?'

'Interesting that you have such a dry sense of humour. You use it to defuse your anxiety.'

She wasn't sure what galled her more: the fact that he could read her so easily, or the fact that she was like this in front of him. Usually she was too closed-off for strangers even to begin to understand her humour. And all this while he hadn't released her, hadn't slowed as they danced around the floor.

'Shall we just forget this conversation,' she asked cheerfully, 'and get on with the night?'

'Why? Am I getting too close for your liking?'

Yes. 'No.'

'I think I am,' he said softly.

She made herself raise her eyebrows at him, as though she was merely amused. As though her heart *wasn't* lodged somewhere in the vicinity of her throat. 'You think altogether too much.'

'And you deflect.'

'Tak…'

Without warning he spun them around, and all she could do was hold on, following his lead the way he'd instructed her to do, praying she didn't trip over her own feet and slowly realising that she was holding her own. Under Tak's unspoken guidance.

The last vestiges of her reticence seemed to melt away. And Tak gauged just the right moment to speak.

'Nell is acting out because she's a thirteen-year-old girl and that's what they do—to a greater or lesser degree. You've just moved home, area, left her friends, and she's feeling like she has no control. The shoplifting was probably a result of peer pressure and bad influence, and she went along with it—even though you've taught her better—because she's trying to exert some kind of dominance but doesn't quite know how. I suspect you already know all of this, because you're clearly a good mother who cares about your daughter.'

'How do you know?'

'The way you've talked about her. The fact that I deal with people day in and day out. I have to operate on them, on their brains—often when they're awake. It pays to be able to read people so you can try to alleviate their deepest fears.'

A myriad of thoughts raced through her head, every one of them too fast for her to catch hold of. 'Yes, I suppose that *would* pay.'

He ignored her, though not unkindly. 'I also suspect you know that what your daughter needs is for you to try talking to her rather than simply punishing her.'

'She can't just get away with it,' Effie objected, refusing to acknowledge that she'd thought pretty much the same thing.

'I didn't say that. Obviously you're going to want to show her that there are consequences—I can see that's who you are, and I don't disagree. I'm just saying don't second-guess your instinct to talk *to* her rather than *at* her. Trust yourself. You're not being a weak mum.'

It was as if he could see right into her thoughts. 'And these consequences?'

He fixed her with an unwavering look. 'That's down to you. You might want to take her back to the shop and face up to them. Pay for the goods.'

'I thought of that, but then I worried that they might prosecute her.'

'It's a possibility, but in my experience they won't. First-time offence…and a teenager taking *one* lipstick? Most likely the staff will appreciate that she's taking responsibility for her mistake and accept her apology and the fact that she's willing to pay for the item.'

It sounded like the ideal solution. However, fear still gnawed at Effie. 'But you can't guarantee that?'

'No, I can't.'

She chewed her lip. 'It might be scary but it's the adult thing to do…'

'And she knows that, or else she wouldn't have told you,' Tak offered. 'She came to you because she isn't happy about it. She wants your help and she needs your understanding.'

'I know that.'

Yet hearing it from him somehow helped her to believe it. He made her feel stronger. This night was turning out to be so very different from anything she might have expected. *Tak* was so very different.

It was a very dangerous realisation indeed.

All he had to do was walk her to her apartment door, then see her inside, and finally leave.

Three steps. *Easy.*

So why had he felt the need to repeat them to himself the entire car journey? As though it was the only way to distract his mind? His body? The way he'd had to do all night.

The effect her proximity had on him had been impossible to ignore. Not least when he'd made the stupid mistake of luring her onto that dance floor in order to haul her into his arms.

Only it hadn't felt like a stupid mistake. It had felt like a fire raging so savagely that he hadn't thought it could ever be smothered. Like a hunger so desperate it had eaten its way through him. Like nothing he'd ever felt before in his entire life.

He'd wanted it never to end.

Tak would never know how he had managed to hold it together on that dance floor, conversing calmly with her whilst his body had been talking itself up into a veritable showdown. He barely remembered much about the rest of the night, save for the fact that Effie had been at his side. Stoking that internal blaze without even realising it.

If it had just been the physical reaction then he could have withstood it. *Couldn't he?* But it had been more than that. It had been that inexplicable emotional connection, too. It had called out to something deep inside him. Reminded him of things he'd once thought best forgotten.

Yet now, finally, the night was almost over and he would soon be released from this pretend date he had never wanted in the first place. However many times he told himself that was a *good* thing, his body seemed determined to protest, its fight only growing stronger.

When the car stopped, he hurried around to let her out himself, and then walked her into the lobby.

'Thank you.' She stopped abruptly. 'I'm fine from here.'

He eyed her obliquely. 'It's late at night. I'll walk you to your door.'

'Really, I'm fine.'

'This isn't up for debate, Effie,' he growled. 'Now, do you want to lead the way or should I carry you?'

She sniffed delicately. 'Don't be ridiculous.'

He didn't recall anyone ever calling him *ridiculous* before. Except perhaps his sister Hetti, and she certainly hadn't said it with the kind of undercurrent that was rippling between Effie and himself right at this moment.

It was intoxicating. And unexpected.

The whole night had been so unpredicted. So voltaic.

He didn't realise they'd reached her apartment until she stopped outside the door and turned to him, her hands playing with each other in that way of hers that he shouldn't already be able to recognise as showing anxiety.

'Well… This is me.' She screwed up her nose. 'Um…thanks for this evening. It was…'

He was too close, he realised belatedly. Too close and too intent. Wholly unable to tear his eyes from the rise and fall of her chest, which betrayed how shallow her breathing was, from her lips and the way her tongue flickered out to moisten them, as though her body knew what it was doing even if her head didn't intend it.

He knew exactly how that felt.

Before he could think twice Tak lowered his head, the fleeting sensation of her hot breath on his chin only charging his body all the more, and claimed her mouth with his own.

He knew he was in big trouble in an instant.

She tasted of lust and longing and pure sensation. All exploding inside him. As if he'd detonated a charge he'd known all along would send him skyrocketing.

He couldn't get enough.

And as her arms looped around his neck, without even the slightest hesitation, and the most delicious of sounds escaped from the back of her throat, he felt as though the whole evening had been building up to this one single moment.

Something rumbled through her, soft and low at first, but as he kissed her and caressed her, sampling her over and over, taking his time and allowing every millimetre of his mouth to become acquainted with every millimetre of hers, it grew louder and more insistent. Tasting, touching, teasing. Angling his head for a better fit and feeling Effie mould her body to his as though by extension. Driving him wild. Heaven and hell all rolled into one. Sweet and sinful, wistful and wild.

He certainly wasn't prepared for Effie to wrench herself away, pushing him back with her palms even as her fingers still gripped his lapels.

'I... That is... You...' She dragged her fingers over her temptingly raw lips incredulously. Her eyes were slightly wide, but still dark with desire. Without warning she swung around, fumbled with her key in the lock, opened the door and finally disappeared inside the flat.

He let her.

He had enough experience with women to know that her head and her body would be at odds with each other right now. If he'd wanted to sway her one way or the other, he could have. But he hadn't, because he wanted her to come to him herself. To beg him to take her. To be sure there was absolutely no doubt in her mind about what she wanted from him.

He pretended not to hear the voice in his head, telling him that this was far removed from what this evening had been *meant* to be about that it made a mockery of their 'buffer' plan. And he let her go even as the sweetness of her mouth still danced on his tongue.

For several long moments he stood, his eyes glued to the closed door, imagining her on the other side, leaning against the wood and struggling to regain her composure.

But before he had a chance to turn around and make his way down the corridor to the elevator, Effie's door abruptly swung open and she pushed straight past him, rushing to the adjacent flat, where she began to wildly hammer on the door.

'Nell? Mrs Appleby? Are you in there?' There was a distinctly frantic edge to her voice.

'Will you calm down? You're going to wake the whole building,' he said.

'They aren't in there.' She jerked her head maniacally, and he could only assume that she was indicating her own flat.

The blaring TV was a good sign. Still, Effie yelled through the door, her voice higher-pitched than ever. 'Mrs Appleby? Is everything—?'

Effie practically toppled inside as the door

swung open without warning, and Tak found himself lurching forward so as not to be shut out.

'You're lucky Mrs Appleby is so deaf that she doesn't realise you're trying to beat down her door,' Nell said, and scowled at her mother before catching sight of Tak. Her eyes narrowed curiously.

If he had any sense of self-preservation at all he would leave. Right now. This wasn't Hetti. Or Sasha. This wasn't his responsibility. This was Nell, and she was Effie's albatross. He prodded himself. Which was why he should already be halfway down the hall.

Instead, Tak folded his arms across his chest and met the kid's bold gaze.

Effie struggled to slow her hammering heart. Though whether it was her panic over the fact that Nell hadn't been where she should have been, or the fact that Tak had been glued to her side since the moment she'd started to freak out, she couldn't be sure.

She didn't think she wanted to analyse it too deeply, anyway.

'Why are you both here?' She turned her attention back to her daughter. 'You're supposed to be in our apartment. You should be in bed.'

'So you've been into the flat?' Nell didn't even attempt to drag her gaze from Tak.

He wouldn't be finding it easy to hold firm,

Effie thought, sucking in a breath. 'Yes. And when you weren't there I got worried. You couldn't have left a note? Some indication that you were here and why?'

'The fact the place is freezing didn't give it away?' Nell retorted, finally dragging her focus back to her mother.

Her young voice held an edge of sarcasm that wouldn't have been there six months ago, but Effie wasn't ready to call her out on it in front of a stranger. Not *this* stranger, anyway.

Had the flat been cold? She hadn't noticed—had only registered the fact that the TV was off—unheard for old Mrs Appleby. Effie wrinkled her nose. In fact she'd been far too preoccupied with that kiss.

It was high time she put that momentary madness behind her. Except that even now her body heated at the memory of what had happened in the hallway with Tak.

Tak's low voice broke into her thoughts. 'Why is your home freezing?'

'The boiler has probably broken down.' Jerking her head up, Effie told herself that there was no need for her to feel ashamed. It was none of his business how they lived.

Her daughter, however, had no such qualms. She eyed Tak. 'It does that a lot.'

'Not a *lot*,' Effie said quickly.

'Oh, come on, Mum. It's all the time.'

'We've only been here three months.'

'And it's the fourth time it's gone.' Nell snorted unapologetically. 'The thing is ancient and you've said it yourself—the landlord is too penny-pinching to replace it.'

'You've called him tonight?' asked Tak suddenly.

'Of course.' Nell pulled a face. 'He said it's the weekend, so the earliest he can get someone out will be Monday, but Tuesday is more likely.'

'Okay—' began Effie, but Tak cut her off.

'Not okay. It's barely spring, it's been a sub-zero winter and there's another cold snap on its way. Repairing your faulty boiler is clearly his top responsibility.'

'As he said, it's the weekend, so that's a reasonable time frame.' At least it was if she didn't want to risk being seen as a troublesome tenant and risk eviction. 'We don't *all* have the kind of money which gets instant action.'

'I'm not challenging your financial circumstances,' he commented unexpectedly. 'I'm neither blind nor stupid. I do understand how putting yourself through medical school at the same time as raising a child must have crippled you.'

'Oh.'

Of all people, she didn't expect Tak to understand so readily. At all, even.

'And I realise you must still be sacrificing to send Nell to that school.'

'It's worth it,' Effie cut in quickly, glowering at him. 'Besides, as soon as I have time to house hunt, I'll be able to find somewhere much better now that I know the area.'

'Effie…'

'Can we just drop it? Please?'

Tak didn't look happy but, ultimately, he obliged.

'So you aren't going to call your landlord again?'

Not quite what she'd meant by 'drop it', but at least he wasn't talking about the school any more. She didn't want Nell uncomfortable at her new school.

'Nell just said she called him.'

'She's *thirteen*.'

'Nell's very responsible.' *If only she'd never mentioned the shoplifting to Tak.*

Her daughter had had to be responsible—it had always been just the two of them. As much as Effie had tried to protect her daughter from growing up too fast, being a single parent and a doctor had nonetheless played its part.

Still, she could be proud of herself that Nell didn't really understand the kind of true ugliness out there that Effie herself had dealt with for most of her childhood. She'd used select parts of her past to teach her daughter how to be strong, confident, and able to think for herself. Yet she'd kept so much of it back—partly out of shame.

'I've no doubt she's extremely responsible...for a thirteen-year-old. Call your landlord.'

It was ridiculous that she found herself squaring her shoulders. 'No.'

There was no way that Tak would understand that calling him a second time would only cause him to push their boiler to the bottom of his list. And she didn't need him—*anyone*—telling her what to do. She would protect her own family the way she always had. She'd got this far on her own, hadn't she?

She threw off the niggling fact that for once—with Tak—she was almost tempted to let someone else in.

'We don't need you swooping in, playing some kind of unwanted superhero. We can sort out our own problems.'

For a long moment they glared at each other.

'Fine.' Tak turned to her daughter abruptly, as though—insultingly—he considered the thirteen-year-old to be the more reasonable of the two of them. 'Give me his number and I'll call him myself.'

'You can't!' Effie gasped.

There would be repercussions if he did. Their landlord wasn't exactly renowned for his understanding nature. And as much as she might be ready to look for a better home as soon as she had some free time, she didn't want them to be kicked out by an irate landlord before she had time to line up somewhere new.

'Wait here,' she instructed, in as firm a voice as she could manage. 'I'll pay Mrs Appleby and then you can argue with me.'

When she got to know the area, and had more than a couple of hours of downtime—hours which were usually spent washing, cleaning and doing the grocery run—then maybe she would have a moment to look for somewhere better.

She found herself shaking the dozing Mrs Appleby awake as gently as possible and thrusting the babysitting payment into the old woman's hand before hurrying out of the flat to catch up with Nell and Tak. Predictably, they hadn't listened to a word of her instructions.

She stood back, chewing her lip, as Tak conducted what seemed like a remarkably one-sided conversation, during which he was doing most of the talking and her usually dominant landlord appeared to be doing an unusual amount of conceding.

'He'll have someone here first thing in the morning,' Tak said, ending the call with something approaching satisfaction. 'You can't spend the weekend with no heating. It's unacceptable.'

'It's called reasonable,' Effie countered. 'At least in *my* world.'

Tak didn't appear remotely swayed. 'I'll wager

that if his own boiler broke down he'd have someone there within the hour.'

'Well, this isn't his flat. It's mine.'

They glared at each other for a long time before Effie finally broke contact, all too acutely aware of Nell's curious gaze.

'Pack a bag,' Tak commanded abruptly. 'You can't stay here.'

It was the crossing of the line in the sand that Effie needed. She rooted herself to the spot and lifted her steady gaze to his. This was *her* daughter, *her* little family, *her* problem. She would deal with it. Just as she always had done.

'Absolutely not.'

'This place is—'

'We're really grateful for you for talking to the landlord,' she said, cutting him off abruptly, 'but we're fine now.'

She didn't know what was galvanising her—she only knew that something was. Perhaps it was the fact that she had long since learned that ultimately people would let you down and she relied only on herself. No one else. Never anyone else.

Not even him.

It was a bit terrifying that the idea of leaning on Tak Basu—even just a little—was so damn tempting. What *was* it about this man that slid through her in a way that no one else ever had? *Ever.*

The next thing she knew she was standing with

her hand on the open door. 'I said that we can take it from here.'

Tak scowled, and looked as though he was about to argue. And then, without warning, he gave a terse nod of his head and strode out. Once in the hallway, he paused long enough to instruct her to call him if she had any more problems and then he was gone.

She chanted over and over in her head, that she was glad.

But even as she closed the door with a flourish, knowing that she would inevitably get the third degree from a barely contained Nell, Effie took a moment to lean her forehead on the cold wood and wonder exactly what she had done.

CHAPTER SIX

'THAT'S IT! THAT'S it—stop!' Effie called to the paramedic to stop chest compressions before shouting to her patient above the noise of the helicopter as it raced through the air. 'Emma, are you with me, sweetheart? You're okay. You're in a helicopter, my love. I'm Effie—I'm a doctor. You're doing well. You're back with us.'

She exchanged a relieved glance with one of her paramedics. It was a hard enough job even without the additional complication of the cramped helicopter space. For several long minutes they continued tending to their patient, before Effie finally sat back on her heels.

'Okay—quick recap. We're back in normal sinus rhythm and she has a line in. We've carried out CPR and one shock, straight up. She's had oxygen, aspirin, no adrenalin.'

The pilot's voice came over the system. 'We're a couple of minutes out from the hospital.'

'Good,' Effie acknowledged, smiling brightly down to her patient, whose eyes were finally open. 'Okay, Emma, we're nearly at the hospital. You've done really well. Now, let's see if we can keep that heart-rate up, shall we?'

For the next half-hour Effie concentrated on the task in hand: keeping her patient comfortable and carrying out her observations before the helicopter finally landed. There wasn't time for her to think about whether or not Tak would be in the resus room when she rushed her patient in. But later—much later—she might acknowledge that deep down there was a tiny part of her which prayed that he wouldn't be there, just as there was another tiny part of her that always hoped he would.

The two parts had been sparring with each other for the last few days.

As they lifted her patient off the helicopter and onto a hospital gurney Effie kept chatting to Emma while the team navigated the long ramp to the hospital. It felt like a win when she finally handed over to the hospital team without Emma going into arrest a second time.

And then there were no distractions or excuses. She was here, in Tak's hospital, and every corner she turned, every corridor she walked, seemed to be a home for ghosts of him.

Had it really only been three days since that night at the gala? Since that kiss? Since he'd seen exactly how she lived? It felt like a lifetime, and if she never had to see him again she would be just fine with that.

She ignored the traitorous part of her which whispered that wasn't true. Just as she pretended that her eyes *weren't* scanning through every door, every window, wondering whether he was just on the other side.

'Are you looking for Tak?'

Effie jumped guiltily as she swung round to see his sister, Hetti. 'Of course not,' she lied brightly. 'I was looking for James, one of my paramedics.'

'Oh.'

She tried not to react to Hetti's all too knowing smile.

'How are you, anyway? How was the ball?'

Effie hesitated 'Good. Yes, fine.'

'You enjoyed it?' Hetti pressed.

'I…yes. Sure. What did Tak say?'

'Not a lot, really,' continued Hetti airily. 'You know Tak.'

But that was the issue, wasn't it? Effie *didn't* know Tak. Not at all, really. Yet she couldn't help thinking that Hetti was watching her a little too closely, as though hoping for a reaction.

'Sure,' she lied, her grin almost painful.

'Having said that,' Hetti added, a little too casually, 'I've never seen him so…shall we say *buoyant*?'

She would not react. She would not.

'Oh. Well. That's good,' she offered brightly. And then she spoiled it all by smoothing her flight suit down as though it was some designer gown. 'Well, I'd better find my paramedic and get back to the heli.'

Hetti practically leapt forward to grab her arm.

'Oh, but…not yet, Effie. There's something I want to ask you.'

'There is?'

'Yes.'

Effie waited patiently.

Hetti clapped her hands and clicked her tongue. 'Yes. There is.'

The moment was eked out until it was almost uncomfortable.

'Well… I really should get going…'

'The thing I want to ask you is…' Hetti shifted awkwardly. Then, as the doors banged at the other end of the corridor, she grinned, exhaled heavily and shook her head and began to hurry the other way. 'Never mind. It'll keep.'

Effie turned away, bemused. And slammed into a solid wall. A warm, *human* solid wall.

She didn't need to see his face to know who it was. A tremor ran through her body like the after-effects of an earthquake.

'Tak.'

'Effie.'

'I've…just been talking with Hetti.'

'So I saw.'

She pursed her lips. 'Did you ask her to stall me?'

If only she wasn't willing him to say yes. Instead he offered a wry smile, and that long, slow ache started up inside her all over again.

'I did not. But I did just receive a call from her saying that she needed me down on this floor.'

So Tak hadn't actually been looking for her. They'd merely been set up. Then again, Tak had come anyway. Was that a good thing or a bad one?

Effie was sure her stomach had no business vaulting and somersaulting the way it was.

'You didn't leave a patient?' she asked feebly.

He eyed her disdainfully. 'Of course not.'

'No,' she cut in hastily. 'Foolish question.'

They stood, the silence stretching uncomfortably between them, whilst Effie tried, and failed, to find something—anything—to say.

'What about the boiler?' He finally broke the silence. 'Did your landlord send someone round the next morning?'

She hesitated as a hundred different thoughts raced through her head. It was barely a beat but it seemed to hang between them for an age, and when she finally spoke her voice was strangled. 'It's in hand.'

'It isn't fixed?' he said sharply.

Another beat.

'It's being fixed.'

'Effie—'

'Actually...' she cut him off hastily '...since you're here, I do owe you a thank-you.'

For a moment, she thought he was going to argue.

'What for?' he ground out instead.

'For Nell. We went to the shop together this morning. You were right—they took one look at her white face, heard her shaky confession and apology, and were more than prepared to let her pay and let her off with a warning because it was her first—and only—time. But they were clear that if they see her in there again with those girls stealing then she won't get off so lightly.'

'And she understood that?'

'I made sure of it.'

She *had* made sure Nell understood. She'd spelled it out in no uncertain terms. But she'd also chatted to her daughter, just as Tak had suggested, and just as she'd known she needed to do all along. And she was confident in her own mind that it had been a stupid, ill-judged, one-time mistake. It wasn't the start of Nell going off the rails.

Not the way she herself had, anyway.

'Am I the first man you've ever taken home, Effie?'

The question came out of nowhere, pulling the proverbial rug out from under her.

'I… Sorry…what does that mean?'

'Exactly what it sounds like.' He sounded amused. 'Am I the first man you've ever taken home?'

'Does it matter?' Not an ideal way to buy herself some time, but it would have to do.

'Only your daughter seemed more curious

about me than perturbed. I wondered if she thought you never dated at all.'

She didn't know whether to be impressed or irritated that he was so astute. 'I date,' she lied, pretending she couldn't hear the defensive note running through her tone.

Because he was right. From the moment she'd lifted her forehead from that cool wooden door that night, to see the sharp gleam in her daughter's eyes, Effie had known something was different. There had been a shift in their mother-daughter relationship, although she couldn't have articulated what that shift was.

Possibly she was hindered by the fact she was still finding it difficult enough trying to process that kiss with Tak—and the fact that even now her body seemed to be aching for it to continue— without dealing with a frowning thirteen-year-old to boot.

'Glad to hear it.'

His reply was so smooth that it took Effie a moment to recall that they'd been talking about whether or not she dated.

'Well…' she declared. 'Um…good.'

It was getting more awkward, more painful by the moment. Yet she couldn't bring herself to move. Which made it all the more humiliating when Tak strode away with apparent ease, talking to her over his shoulder.

'Okay, then, if that's all you wanted me for I should get back to work.'

'I *didn't* want you. Hetti wanted you,' Effie managed at last.

But it was too late. He was already gone and she was left to make her way back to the helicopter, her head now full of memories of Nell's none too subtle interrogation the night of the ball.

'Who was the guy?' her daughter had demanded without preamble.

She might have known Nell wouldn't easily let it go. 'No one,' she'd ventured.

Her daughter had scoffed in the way that only teens could. 'Is he your boyfriend?'

Effie remembered opening her mouth to answer, but then catching herself. What kind of example was it to set for her thirteen-year-old daughter? She had been kissing someone who had, when it came down to it, been more of a ride to the gala than anything else. Or at least he was supposed to have been.

So she'd fibbed. 'He was my date but… I don't know if we'll be seeing each other again.'

For a long moment her daughter had eyed her without answering, whilst Effie had tried to pretend to herself that she didn't secretly wish it really *had* been a date. Her first one in years.

When Nell had finally spoken, it hadn't been at all what Effie had been expecting.

'Was it a bad date?' she'd asked, her voice

softer than anything Effie had heard from her in a long while. Sympathetic. 'Did he flirt with another girl? I was on a date with Adam Furnisson, but all he did was flirt with Greta Matthews the whole time. It was…humiliating.'

A date? Nell? When the hell had that happened?

Effie had bitten her tongue so hard that she was sure, even now, she could still taste blood. But demanding the details would have only made her daughter shut her out again.

She'd never even heard those names before. How was it that an unexpected kiss with Tak—the kind that had probably meant nothing to him but which had shaken her so—had put her back into a position where her daughter suddenly wanted to confide in her again?

She'd had to choose her words carefully when she'd warned Nell that, 'If a boy treats you like that then he simply isn't worth it.'

Nell had twisted her mouth in a way which had suggested she knew that in her head but her innocent neo-teen heart was having some difficulty with the concept.

'I know…' She'd blown out a deep breath. 'But it's Adam *Furnisson*, Mum. He's, like…the hottest guy in school, and it's a big deal to even be part of his squad.'

Oh, to love a child and yet simultaneously want to strangle them.

Tak's words had come back to her unexpectedly and for a moment they had helped to take some of the heat out of Effie's instinctive response. What else had Tak said...? That maybe she should try talking to her daughter? Well, it was worth a try.

Hesitantly, she'd taken her daughter's hand and led her to the sofa, promising to make them a hot drink and have a chat. *Like grown-ups.*

Nell's eyes had begun to narrow suspiciously, but then she'd offered a surprised, pleased, but wary nod, before following her mother across the room.

To Effie it had felt like the kind of victory she couldn't even have dreamed of a few hours before. Before Tak. Before his advice.

Yet with his words resounding in her head—his assurance that she was doing a good job and his instruction to give herself a break—she'd felt a renewed confidence to tackle Nell. And the rest of her conversation with her daughter, including about the shoplifting, had followed from there.

None of it had been ground-breaking. It had just been everything she should have known for herself. Probably *did* know, deep down. But somehow, somewhere along the line, she'd lost confidence in herself and begun second-guessing the way she was with her own daughter.

It made her wonder exactly how Tak had understood the situation so well.

And what was it that made Hetti so very protective and fiercely proud of her brother? Because it was more than just the fact that he was a renowned neurosurgeon.

Suddenly Effie was more than keen to find out.

It had taken Tak hours of ward rounds, surgery and ultimately hated paperwork for Tak to finally push Effie out of his head. Even when he was focussed on his job she still lurked there. Somewhere in the back of his subconscious.

He was sure she had been lying about the repair to the boiler in her flat being *in hand.*

Taking the stairs two at a time—always faster than waiting for the hospital elevators at this time of day—Tak thrust all thoughts from his head. It shouldn't matter to him. They weren't his business. Not Effie. Not her daughter. Not their boiler.

Effie had been a means to an end—as he had been for her—a mutually convenient arrangement for one night only. There was absolutely no reason for him to think about her any more. No reason for him to tell himself he needed to find something to douse this *thing* that was simmering dangerously inside him.

It had almost been a relief when he'd managed to walk away back there in the hospital corridor. He'd managed to break the spell Effie had unknowingly woven around him.

Yet he couldn't shake the memory of the way

she'd watched him. With a look approaching dis-appointment in her eyes. And something else, too. Something altogether too much like hurt.

Consequently, the last thing he expected was to get an emergency call from Resus, patching through a familiar, if crackly voice from the air ambulance.

'Effie?'

Had she called just to talk to him?

'Tak?'

The shocked tone was too palpable to miss. Clearly she hadn't asked for him by name.

And then she shook off her shock and plunged in. 'I'm with a casualty—forty-year-old female. Road traffic accident. GCS six. Pupils uneven with left pupil dilated and fixed. Infrascanner showed a subdural haematoma.'

'So get her in to me,' he barked.

'We can't,' she replied simply. 'We're not cleared to fly. There's been an explosion and there's thick, black smoke around us so we can't see to fly out and no one can see to get to us right now.'

He processed the scenario in moments. This patient needed surgery to alleviate the pressure on her brain. A delay of mere hours could result in permanent brain injury. Which meant someone needed to do it out in the field. *Now.*

A tiny part of him was relieved that it was Effie on the other end of the phone rather than anyone else. But he could process that bit of information later. In his own time.

'You're going to need to perform an emergency burr hole evacuation.'

'Yes.'

That quiet, calm affirmation was like the final puzzle piece slotting in. Any residual doubts Tak had dissipated quietly.

'Okay—the patient is intubated?'

'Yes, and in a C-spine.'

'You're going to need a knife, a drill, swabs, a self-retainer... Saline should ideally be hypertonic...'

'Tak, we're not an emergency department or an operating room. We've got some kit on board, but the rest is mix and match and DIY stuff. I really need you to talk me through it.'

'Okay, give me your mobile number and I'll call you back on it. And I'll send you an image showing the standard position of burr holes, which you're going to need to modify depending on what the Infrascanner shows.'

He grabbed a pen and jotted down the number she gave him, replaced the department phone and headed for a quiet room as he sent her the image.

He called her back.

'Tak?'

She picked up on the first ring, her nerves controlled but nonetheless evident. He didn't blame her.

'You'll be fine.' He kept his tone as brisk as he could. 'I'll talk you through it as we go, but here's a summary. You're going to need to shave about a five-centimetre strip of hair. Then you'll mark a three-centimetre incision and clean the area, preferably with chlorhexidine. You'll make an incision right down to the bone, controlling any bleeding with direct pressure.'

'Understood.'

She had to be nervous but she was mastering it, which boded well for the casualty. His respect for Effie hitched up yet another notch.

'You're going to need to use either the knife or a swab to push the periosteum off the bone, and ideally this is when you'd insert the self-retaining retractor. Or whatever it is you've got.'

'Right,' she confirmed.

'Now comes the hard part. The drill *must* be perpendicular to the skull, and you're going to need one of your paramedics to hold the casualty's head and apply saline as you drill. Effie, you're going to have to push down hard, and once you've started drilling *keep* drilling until the drill bit stops spinning. If you stop too soon it's going to disengage the mechanism and make it that much harder to start again.'

'Understood,' she said again.

Her grim tone crackled over the connection, and he could imagine she had swallowed. Pretending she didn't feel sick with adrenalin as it coursed wildly around her veins. She needed it to. There was no way she was going to get through this unless she was fired up enough.

But still, as he outlined the rest of the procedure and then waited for her to ensure everything was in place before beginning to talk her through it step by step, it occurred to Tak that there was no other doctor he would rather have on the end of the line right now. No one else he would trust to perform such a procedure whilst they waited for either a road ambulance to get to them or for clearance to fly the heli out with the patient.

This was so much worse than just a physical attraction. It seemed he liked and admired Effie, too. When had anyone *ever* got to him like this? When had this constant awareness *ever* shot through him? It was an awareness which flared into something infinitely more palpable—more forceful—every time he saw her. Even spoke to her.

The woman's nature was as fiery and captivating as her glorious red hair.

Just like that, an image locked itself in his mind. So detailed that she might as well have been standing right in front of him. Her lilting voice, her delicate fragrance, the way her skin felt so soft and yet so electric beneath his fingers. And as for the way she'd tasted when his mouth had plundered hers…the way she had given herself up to him as though they had been the only two people to ever to kiss that way in the history of the world…

It made no sense.

Neither did the way his whole body combusted at the mere memory. As though he was the untried, untested boy of his youth rather than a man who had enjoyed his fair share of sexual encounters.

It was bizarre. But not altogether unpleasant.

Although it *was* inconvenient.

Which could mean only one thing. He really was in deep trouble.

CHAPTER SEVEN

'WHAT ARE YOU doing here?' she asked testily, thirteen hours later, as he found himself hammering on her apartment door.

His gaze swept down, taking in her multiple layers of jumpers, and the expression in his eyes hardened.

'The boiler hasn't been repaired at all. You lied to me.'

She bristled instantly. 'I did not lie.'

'You told me it was repaired.'

'No, I told you it was in hand. Which it is.'

'I hardly see how,' he remarked dryly. 'Unless you're trying to recreate the Arctic Tundra in there.'

Effie wasn't sure what took her aback the most. The fact that they were sparring about this, on her doorstep, or the fact that they were sparring at all. Surely it didn't matter to him one way or another whether one of his colleagues had heating in their home or not?

More than that, there was the fact that something had changed between them. So subtle that she couldn't exactly put her finger on what it was, but there seemed to be a deeper affinity there now.

Then again, he had very recently talked her

through drilling a burr hole into a brain at the roadside. Surely that had to alter any relationship?

Still, she couldn't stop her eyes from flickering over his shoulder and along the corridor beyond. If Mrs Appleby saw him—again—the rumour mill would really start cranking up.

'If that's what you came for, perhaps you should now go.'

There was no justification for the way her mouth fought against her uttering the words. Or for the way her heart skipped so merrily when he didn't move. If anything, he seemed to root his feet to the cracked hallway floor all the more.

'It isn't what I came for.'

'Then what?'

It was almost indiscernible, his hesitation, as if he was trying to think quickly of something to say. But then he continued and Effie realised she must have imagined it.

'I thought you might like to know how your first brain surgery patient is.'

She was torn. A sense of self-preservation warred with the professional side of her, which ached to know that she hadn't caused any harm to her RTA casualty.

'She's okay? I did okay?'

His mouth curved softly at one corner. 'You did okay,' he confirmed. 'Better than okay. You saved her life.'

'Thanks to you, talking me through it so concisely.'

Pride whooshed through her, making her feel at least ten feet tall. She couldn't control the smile as it took her over her face, her eyes locking with Tak's. For a moment he looked as though he was about to say more, but then changed his mind.

'Obviously. Now, if you don't want the whole building buzzing about the strange man on your doorstep, perhaps you should let me in.'

She ought to refuse, stand her ground. Instead she found her fingers reaching for the bolt, her hand shaking a little too much with eagerness.

'Hurry up.' Agitation and excitement vied for supremacy in her tone. 'Before someone sees you.'

The temperature hit him the moment he entered.

'It's really is like the tundra in here.'

It sounded more like an accusation than a comment. It was all she could do to eye him with disapproval. No doubt he wouldn't be used to that. When was the last time anyone had eyed Tak Basu with anything other than approval? Admiration? *Lust?*

She pushed that thought out of her head in an instant. 'Why are you here, Tak?'

'Did the repair guy even turn up?'

'Tak—'

'Did he turn up?' he interrupted.

She glared at him. 'Yes.'

'But he didn't repair it?'

'Oh, he did.' She narrowed her eyes. 'But Nell and I don't use it because we *like* it this cold.'

'Why didn't he repair it?' Tak chose to ignore her sarcasm.

She tried to out-glare him, but when she saw that clearly wasn't going to work she finally relented with a sigh. 'It seems it's a little complicated.'

'How complicated?'

'The boiler is on its last legs. It needs to be replaced. But a new boiler won't connect to the old system. I'm not entirely sure, but I think it's something about microbore pipework. They need to run in a fresh central heating line.'

He nodded, as though he understood what she was saying. Which didn't really surprise her.

'And how long will that take?'

'A few weeks. Maybe.'

'A few *weeks*?' Tak was disparaging. 'It's a small flat, surely a week would suffice?'

'As I understand it, they think they will need to take down at least one ceiling from the building plant room above, access at least one wall void, and then certainly take up every floor covering, floor board and re-lay all new pipework. Without disturbing any of my neighbours in the building. Even a layperson like me can see that could take a while.'

'I see. And where does this landlord of yours expect you—and all your belongings, to live during this period?'

'Here,' she tried for a nonchalant shrug 'They can work in one or two rooms at a time so we can move around with them.'

'Then forget a few weeks! If they're stop-starting like that to work around you—and your furniture—then that could take a month. Longer, even.'

'I guess…' She shrugged. 'But that's just how it is. At least we still have somewhere to live.'

'And you just accepted that? For pity's sake, Effie, can't you see that your landlord is walking all over you?'

'Probably—but what can I do about it? There's nothing in my tenancy agreement stating that the landlord is legally obliged to find us alternative accommodation. If I shout and rage then he'll only take it out on us in an even worse way.'

She'd thought it would help, but her calmness only seemed to creep under his skin all the more. As if her acceptance made him feel as though he needed to shout louder, fight harder on her behalf.

Or maybe that was just because she wanted him to.

It made no sense. She'd long since given up expecting anyone else to fight her battles, or even stand beside her whilst she fought them herself. She'd wanted someone to do that for her, her whole life. But they hadn't. Except for that one time, but look how that had turned out.

'No, that's unacceptable.'

Effie blinked, barely recognising Tak's voice. It sounded odd, somehow. Tight. A little like her smile felt as she twisted her mouth into some semblance of one. Something was bugging him. She couldn't explain why that pleased her, but it did.

'It's unfortunate, I'll grant you, but it's just the way it is.'

'I won't accept it.'

His words were sharp, edgy. She could almost see them cutting the air. Something sloshed inside her.

'What are you going to do? Repair it yourself? After having conjured the obsolete spare parts out of thin air, of course. We all know you're a superhero surgeon, of course, but I didn't realise your expertise stretched to boilers and central heating as well.'

A hundred thoughts were racing through Tak's head at that moment. She could see them but she couldn't grasp a single one of them. And the way he was watching her… It made it impossible for her to explain this dark thing which fogged her head and swirled in eddies around her chest.

'You can't stay here.'

His voice was too thick. It *did* things to her. She could almost *feel* her smile. It was sharp, edgy, so un-Effie-like.

'And yet here I am.'

'What about your daughter?' he challenged, and her non-smile disappeared in a flash. 'It's like living inside a freezer.'

'You think I don't know that? But where else should I stay? I could stay at the hospital, but I can't take Nell, and I can't afford a hotel.'

'You'll stay with me.'

'No!' Effie exclaimed, a shrill note of panic echoing through her voice.

'Effie, what does it tell your daughter that you're putting up with this landlord messing you around? Taking advantage?'

He might not have intended it, but what he'd said played on every insecurity she had.

'I don't need someone to swoop in and save me,' she growled. 'I've been taking care of my daughter alone for thirteen years. I don't need a...a...stranger telling me he knows best.'

'For pity's sake, this isn't some test as to whether you're a good mother or not,' he countered. 'Are you trying to tell me that you *aren't* both absolutely freezing and miserable?'

She clenched and unclenched her fists at her sides. 'We can cope. We've put up with worse.'

'I don't doubt it—more's the pity!'

His voice was too even, too level, and somehow that got under her skin all the more. Her temper—which she'd kept hidden away for more years than she could remember—began to flare.

'We don't need you charging in thinking we need saving. Offering us your goodwill like we're some charity case. Suggesting we can't manage.'

'It wasn't an offer,' he replied grimly. 'Or a suggestion.'

'Really?' Effie could barely contain her incredulity. 'You're *that* high-handed you think you can just *order* me and my thirteen-year-old daughter to come and stay with you and I'll obey? As if that doesn't set a worse example to her than anything else?'

'Fine.' His jaw pulled taut. 'Then I'm at least calling the creep to find out exactly what's going on.'

She couldn't possibly have articulated what it was in his expression that rooted her to the spot. That made her whole body shiver so deliciously despite everything. And before she could analyse it further he'd turned from her, pulling out his mobile phone. It was only when he began speaking that she realised with whom he was having his rather commanding one-sided conversation.

Goodness, he must have saved the number when Nell had given him their landlord's contact details. She should react. Stop him. Grab the phone and take control. Awkwardly, stiffly, she reached her hand out, but abruptly his face darkened menacingly as he growled into the phone.

'Asbestos?'

Effie froze solid. She was watching and listening, but unable to move or to say a word. Her brain was apparently not even capable of understanding Tak's side of the conversation, save for the fact that she would be eternally grateful his barely contained rage wasn't remotely directed at her.

Finally, he terminated the call with a grim sound. All she could do was wait. Immobile. Barely even breathing.

'It seems your flat is located directly below the plant room,' he bit out at length. 'It seems that since the last conversation, he found asbestos in the lagging around the pipes. It's going to need to be cleared out immediately—which means taking your ceiling down to get to the pipes.'

She felt as though she was fighting to swim through treacle. 'Okay, but that won't take long, surely? It's a small flat. Pulling out a bit of insulation might take a day? Two?'

'They'll have to remove the ceilings from your entire flat, clear out the lot, re-insulate, board the ceilings, then plaster then. You're talking a minimum of a week. Then there's still the week or so to replace all the pipework in your flat.'

'Two weeks?' it would eat up all her savings, and then some.

'It isn't just that, Effie. Your landlord is going to need surveys, HSE approval, and then find a fully licensed contractor to remove the asbestos. You're talking a minimum of six weeks—and that's assuming he can find someone available to start straight away.'

The ramifications came at her almost in slow motion. 'Nell and I are going to have to move out?' Her voice didn't even sound like her own.

'Yes.'

'For six weeks?'

'At least.'

'No!' Effie exclaimed, unable to cover the note of panic in her tone. 'How dare you? You...you've no right.'

There was a note in her voice which threatened to betray the fact that it wasn't just her pride talking, but rather her flip-flopping traitorous heart. A note which gave away just how wickedly tempting his offer was.

'I didn't create this, Effie.' He sounded unperturbed. 'I didn't put the asbestos there.

'No right to meddle!' she cried. 'You called him. You pushed him.'

'Which meant he told the truth *now* instead of in a few days or weeks.'

'And it's just my flat?'

'No, it's all three flats on this floor.'

Her stomach somersaulted. 'Oh, no—Mrs Appleby!'

'Apparently, she's going to stay with her sister, a few hours' drive away. I don't know about the other flat's occupants.'

What did it say about her that she didn't even know their names?

'I have no idea where we can go,' she whispered, more to herself than anyone else.

'Like I said. You'll stay with me. Only this time I'm not offering.'

Effie didn't miss the edge to his voice, but her mind was too busy reeling for her to be able to take it on board fully.

'Anyway, my home is expansive enough that we could live in separate wings and not even see or hear each other.'

She hesitated. What other choice did she have? And why couldn't she shake the part of her which was secretly revelling in this horrible turn of events?

'Really?'

'Unless you *want* us to see each other, of course.'

It was an attempt at a joke, she was pretty sure, but they were both too tense to laugh. The air was so fraught she was almost suffocating. And then something lurched inside her chest that she pretended not to notice.

She tilted her head a fraction higher. 'You're funny,' she said, her voice cracked.

'Did you just chin-check me?'

He grinned suddenly. It was a stunning, heart-stopping sight. And incredibly, impossibly, everything simply *shifted*.

'Why are you being so nice, anyway?' Effie

valiantly fought to eye his obscenely tantalising grin with something she hoped approached disdain. 'What's in it for you?'

'Would it make it easier for you if there was something?'

Would it? Probably.

She lifted her shoulders as casually as she dared. 'Maybe.'

He laughed. A warm, rich sound which seemed to seep through her very bones like the sun on a gorgeously hot day.

'Fine. Then what if I told you that my extended family have backed off on the whole arranged marriage idea since word got back to them about me being at the gala with you.'

She *didn't* feel a tingle ripple through her. *She didn't.*

'Is that so?'

'It is.'

She waited for him to elaborate but he didn't. He was deliberately waiting for her to probe him. To show her hand. She wanted to hold her nerve, but curiosity won out—as galling as that was.

'Go on, then. I'll bite. *Why* isn't your mother insisting on an arranged marriage any more?'

'I guess because her endgame is for me to provide her with grandchildren. Whether she sets me up or I meet a future wife on my own terms is really neither here nor there to her.'

She could feel his words all over her. Sliding

over her skin and slinking through her veins. He hadn't meant it like that, but she couldn't stop hearing the words echoing in her head, over and over...

His future wife. As if it could be her. As if she *wanted* it to be her.

She'd spent her whole life certain that she would never want that. People let each other down and betrayed each other—that was just human nature. They only wanted to know another person if there was something in it for themselves.

Except, perhaps, a very rare few—like Eleanor Jarvis, the closest thing Effie had ever had to a loving maternal figure. And look what had happened to *her.*

'What about sex?' she asked abruptly.

'Are you offering?'

That sinful curve of his mouth was almost her undoing. *'No!'*

'Relax. I'm teasing. No sex.'

'And kissing?'

She hoped her cheeks didn't flush as she recalled the spine-tingling kiss they'd shared outside her apartment door that night.

'Not even a superficial air-kiss,' he answered solemnly.

She narrowed her eyes. It sounded suspiciously as if he was teasing her.

'Good,' she offered at last.

She didn't even sound as if she believed herself. But if Tak wanted to offer her and Nell a roof over their heads, as long as his gain wasn't their downfall surely she could live with that?

'*This* is where he lives?' Nell whispered beside her as they both stood outside the house, staring up in undisguised shock. Suddenly she sounded small and...thirteen.

Their argument during the drive over here had been momentarily forgotten and Effie was grateful. She wasn't sure she had the energy for dealing with living in Tak's home as well as for another full-scale debate on why she was refusing to let her daughter attend the birthday party of a girl Effie had never met before.

Fortunately, the sight of the former seemed to have rather knocked the latter into the dirt, and Nell kept on staring up, her hand moving to clutch her mother's arm.

Effie didn't blame her. The place was imposing. Unquestionably huge and unfeasibly stunning. And yet somehow it was also surprisingly inviting.

How it achieved that Effie couldn't quite be sure, but the arresting building seemed to ooze the personality of its owner through every substantial wall, every imposing sheet of glass and every single breathtaking view of the lush countryside.

'It's like...like a castle or something.'

It wasn't. For a start it was far too modern, too sleek. But Effie could understand what her daughter meant. To a girl who had been brought up with as few material goods as Effie had been able to give her this must seem like something out of a fairy tale.

Heck, if it hadn't been for the unwelcome memories flooding her brain even to *her* it would have felt like something unbelievably enchanting and idyllic. But instead her stomach heaved and churned.

She felt like a thirteen-year-old herself, although *her* reactions were a lot more emotionally charged than her daughter's. How many times had she stood in a stranger's hallway, a battered duffel bag—which she'd held onto because somehow it reminded her of where she'd come from, and how hard she'd struggled to get to where she was now—in her hand, staring around at another person's home and plastering a stiff smile on her lips in gratitude that they were deigning to let her into it.

'It can't *all* be his, Mum. I bet they're luxury apartments and he just has one of them.'

Effie didn't agree, but before she could say anything the front door swung open. A man stood on the doorstep, looking down on them. He was about fifty years old, perhaps sixty, in a dark, neat suit, his shoes polished to within an inch of their lives, and his face neutral. Some might say carefully so.

'Dr Robinson? And this must be Miss Robinson.'

It took Effie a moment to realise that she should step forward. 'Um…yes. That's right. You can call me Effie, and this is Nell. And you are Mr Havers?'

'Just Havers,' he stated crisply. 'Now, *Dr Robinson*, allow me to show you and Miss Robinson around—unless you'd prefer to go directly to your wing? Mr Basu hopes that you will be comfortable here.'

'Our *wing*?' Nell whispered at her side as Havers gestured to invite them in. 'It really is just one big house?'

'Leave your luggage over there. I'll see that it's taken upstairs.'

'Thank you.' Effie gritted her teeth, cringing inwardly—their bags were hardly the designer luggage she suspected most women visiting this place used—and headed inside.

The tour progressed in a blur of one incredible space after another, so vast that her head was already beginning to spin and she had the impression that they were barely halfway through. It was a blessing and a curse when she heard footsteps tapping up the wooden hallway behind her and knew, without even turning around, that it would be Tak.

No one else made her body...*prickle* quite the way that he did. Right then she determined that she wouldn't turn around.

'Ah, there you are, Havers. Is it all going well?'

'Mr Basu!'

The genuine warmth in the older man's smile caught Effie by surprise.

'I wasn't expecting you back so soon. I thought this was your evening with your brother?'

'I'm sure Rafi can manage without me for one week. Besides, I thought I could finish the tour myself—no doubt you have plenty of other work you'd rather be getting on with.'

'As you wish.' The older man nodded sagely and began to take a step away.

Was it panic or something else that made Effie spin around in an instant? Either way, it was calamitous the way her heart clashed with her head in that moment. She was grateful that her head won out. Just.

'We're fine with Mr...with Havers,' she retorted primly.

But at exactly the same time her daughter boldly accepted Tak's offer.

'Then let us continue.' Tak grinned at Nell as though Effie herself hadn't even spoken.

And then her thirteen-year-old daughter straightened her shoulders and looked her host in the eye, as though she wasn't remotely intimidated by him or the situation. As though her momentary lapse into awe had never happened.

'We're fine,' Effie echoed, a little hollowly. 'We've seen enough already. We don't need to intrude on the rest of your home.'

'We do if we don't want to get lost,' Nell objected.

'We won't get lost.'

Her daughter's snort wasn't the most ego-boosting of responses.

'Let's be fair, Mum, you're geographically backward. Don't you remember that estate we lived on a few years ago? It took you almost ten months to work out which way led to the supermarket and which way led to the motorway.'

'The roads all looked the same,' Effie muttered.

Tak chuckled loudly. There was no reason at all for that smooth sound to ripple over her as it did.

Nell continued, oblivious. 'And here the corridors all look the same.' She blew out a faintly triumphant breath. 'So all the more reason to learn the layout. You don't want to go wandering into Tak's bedroom thinking it's your own, do you?'

Fire rushed through her and Effie yanked her head up sharply, but her daughter's expression was wholly innocent. Either Nell had a better poker face at thirteen than Effie herself had ever possessed, or she genuinely hadn't intended to sound so inappropriate.

Effie chose to believe the latter. Still, she couldn't stop her gaze sliding to Tak. Wondering if he'd caught on. Hoping that somehow he hadn't.

'We certainly can't have that, can we?'

His amusement was palpable, as though he was reading her mind. And that voice, as rich and indulgent as ever, meant the undercurrents inside her only sloshed around her all the more turbulently.

She straightened her spine. 'No, we cannot.'

Too prim. Too uptight. But too late now.

'So you live here all alone? Just you?'

'My other sister Sasha and my brother Rafi used to live here before they each got married, which was nice…' Tak shrugged, but his voice held that soft note she'd heard once before at the ball. 'But now it's mainly just me and Hetti.'

And then the moment was gone and Tak was smiling down at Nell.

'Anyway, what do you want to see next?' Tak grinned down at Nell. 'The cinema room, the pool, or the games den?'

There was no mistaking Nell's expression of awe, even if it *was* smothered in as neutral an expression as a thirteen-year-old girl could muster.

'What's in the games den?' Nell demanded with a grin of her own.

'Pool table, football table, two-lane bowling alley, some arcade machines.'

Nell's attempt at teenage blasé acceptance crumbled in an instant.

'Of course there is! You could fit our flat into this place ten times over. At least. You're so lucky, having a games room that you don't have to share with anyone else. You must be, like, a gazillionaire!'

'*Nell!*'

Instantly her daughter mumbled an apology, but Tak merely laughed.

'It isn't about that. My life is being a doctor—a surgeon. I don't always get enough time off and when I do it might not be the most sociable hours. Sometimes it's nice to have a place to come and wind down, even if it's four in the morning.'

'Chillax.' Nell nodded sagely. 'Mum could do with more of that.'

'*Mum* doesn't always have time for that,' Effie interjected pointedly, wishing they would stop talking about her as though she wasn't even there.

Not that it made much difference as she traipsed politely down a sweeping metal staircase and into a basement area. Tak swung open the door and both Nell and Effie were helpless to contain their shock.

It was like something out of those 'millionaires' cribs' shows her daughter was addicted to watching. All coloured LED strip-lighting, white stone floors and lots and lots of man-toys.

Table games dominated one zone: a pool table

and table football, air hockey and table tennis. Arcade machines dominated another, with racing motorbikes and basketball hoops. A two-lane bowling alley ran the length of one side, and a full-size snooker table stood proudly in a section of its own.

Nell turned abruptly to eye Effie. 'I guess this is what you could have had if you'd just concentrated on your career and hadn't had to raise a baby all by yourself.'

'Not at all,' Effie choked, emotions rushing at her so violently that it was all she could do not to take a step back, as though that might somehow ward them off.

'The way she talks about you I can't imagine that your mother would trade you for any of... *this*.' Tak waved his hand around dismissively. 'You're the most important thing in her life—anyone can see that. And you must know that the only reason she's come here is because she's thinking about what's best for you. She would have suffered that igloo you call home indefinitely if it had just been her!'

There was a beat, then Nell scuffed her canvas shoe against the pristine stone floor. But all Effie could do was stare at the back of the head of this man—this relative stranger—who she was pretty sure she'd just heard defending her.

She told herself it meant nothing.

Inside her chest a heavy drum tattoo suggested otherwise.

'I know,' Nell muttered eventually. 'She's always put me first.'

Tak's smile was surprisingly soft. 'She's also your fiercest advocate.'

'Yeah, I know that too. Even if she can be a bit of a walk-over in other areas.'

'I am *not* a walk-over,' Effie spluttered.

The pair ignored her, as though they were banding together to disprove her point without either of them saying a word.

It was the oddest sensation in the word. Nell and Tak, clicking together as if they'd known each other for years, not merely met on two brief occasions. Something swept through Effie and it took her a moment to realise it was regret tinged with perhaps a hint of guilt.

In trying to protect the two of them all these years—trying to do her best for her daughter—was it possible she had been wrong to deprive Nell of any male presence in her life? A role model if not a father figure?

Not Tak, of course, that would be bonkers—true bats in the belfry, as Eleanor would have said. But someone. There had been enough date offers over the years, even from men who had known she had a child.

Had she been selfish in not even trying? Claiming to be protecting her daughter from people dropping in and out of her life when actually she'd been protecting herself?

Effie shook her head almost imperceptibly and pulled her shoulders back. *No, she hadn't been selfish*. The simple truth was that no man had ever appealed to her enough for her to *want* to risk opening her life up for them. They hadn't been enough.

'Right.'

Tak's voice broke into her reverie.

'You've seen your wing and the main areas of the house. I'll leave you to settle in at your own pace. Havers is around if you need anything.'

And then he was gone, and Effie was staring at the doorway as though it might bring him back. It seemed all she had to do now was ignore the needling voice in her head pointing out to her that none of those men had been Tak Basu.

'You aren't going.' Effie was determined to remain steadfast, however torn she felt internally. 'It's a school night.'

It had been two days since Tak had left them to settle in. True to his word, their paths hadn't crossed since then, although between Havers and the rest of the staff she and Nell hadn't ever felt alone in the vast house.

But still, it was hard not to feel that their every move was being witnessed by someone. Especially when they were arguing.

As if to prove Effie's point, Nell glowered at her in disbelief. 'But it's her *birthday*.'

'So you already said. Several times.'

'I thought you *wanted* me to make friends,' Nell threw out, making no attempt to hide her frustration. 'You're the one who upended our lives by dragging us here.'

She shouldn't bite back—she knew that—but whether her daughter realised it or not it was a low blow. Guilt scraped at her. She *had* uprooted her daughter, she *was* always telling Nell she had to make new friends, and yet she *did* stop her from going anywhere on school nights.

Despite herself, Effie vacillated—and that lent her voice a sarcastic note she would have preferred it not to have. 'Yes, I'm *sorry* that getting a new job that earns more money and gives us a few luxuries has interfered with your social life.'

Nell tipped her nose into the air with all the authority of a teenager who knows everything. 'It's not just about money, Mum.'

'Says the thirteen-year-old who has never understood the fear of receiving an eviction notice.'

'My God, you're being unreasonable.'

'Who's being unreasonable?' Tak asked, sauntering into the kitchen as though Effie and Nell's rather public argument didn't perturb him in the slightest.

'I'm sorry. I didn't realise you were back from the hospital. We'll leave you in peace.'

'*Mum's* being unreasonable,' Nell announced, ignoring her.

'I'm sorry, this really doesn't have anything to do with you—' Effie began, but she was drowned out by an indignant Nell.

'There's a girl at school and it's her birthday party tonight. A group of girls are going bowling at that big place just outside of town? You know—looks like your games suite downstairs, only bigger, and with a lot more people? Anyway, she's invited me, even though I'm new. It's a really big deal.'

Effie opened her mouth to respond, but Tak nudged her discreetly. She turned to him with a frown and then, although she couldn't explain why, decided to trust him.

'Are these the same girls you went shoplifting with?'

'You *told* him?' Nell swung around to her mother, her face on fire.

But once again Tak answered before Effie could say a word.

'Of course she did. She had to.' He shrugged calmly, as though it was obvious. 'Surely you know there are always consequences to your actions, Nell? I've opened up my home to you—it would have been wrong of her not to mention it.'

For several long seconds Nell continued to scowl at her. Then, to Effie's surprise and pride, she smoothed her face into an expression of acceptance and nodded. 'Yes, I know. And I am truly sorry for stealing. For what it's worth, I'll never make that mistake again.'

'That's good to hear,' Tak replied graciously. 'Nell, would you excuse your mother and I for a moment?'

Effie watched in shock as Nell nodded again, then obediently left the room. If it had been just herself and her daughter she knew Nell would have been like a dog with the proverbial bone.

CHAPTER EIGHT

'YOU'RE REALLY AGAINST her going?' Tak's low voice broke across Effie's thoughts as soon as the door clicked shut.

'I can guarantee I'm not the only mum who would be worried if she didn't know her daughter's new friends. In fact, I happen to know that a couple of the other mums are actually going. But I'm working. And I can't just change shifts at the air ambulance.'

Still, her conscience pricked her, as it seemed to be doing more and more these days. If this was what the next few years were going to be like with her daughter then she didn't think she could stand it.

'I'm just lucky that Havers is here and has generously promised to look after Nell the way Mrs Appleby does when she gets home from school.'

'So you aren't averse to Nell attending the party in general?' Tak asked suddenly.

'Of course not. Contrary to what you might have overheard before you walked in, I *do* actually want my daughter to make friends.'

'I know that,' he replied evenly.

Effie swallowed. She couldn't put her finger on what it was about the way he was looking at her, but in an instant the room seemed to fade away.

'This…this isn't about me,' she managed.

'I'll take that as confirmation.'

'Take it however you want,' she shot back, but even she could hear there was no heat in her tone. 'This is about Nell and whether I'm deliberately stopping her from going to a party.'

'And you're adamantly trying to show that you aren't?'

'Of course I'm not,' Effie bristled. 'If I knew she was going to be safe that would be different. But I don't know any of these girls and I can't be there because of work.'

'In that case, what if *I* took Nell to the party?'

It was surreal. Effie stared at Tak, unsure what to say. Was he really offering to parent her child, reasoning with her as though it was the most natural thing in the world?

'I don't think it's a good idea,' she said slowly. 'I mean, people might get the wrong impression.'

'You mean, people might actually think there's something going on between you and I?' Tak rolled her eyes. 'As if the fact you're staying here doesn't already do that?'

There was no reason her heart should be slamming into the wall of her chest like this.

Effie sucked in a deep breath, not that it helped. 'We're only staying here until our central heating is fixed and the asbestos is removed.' But she floundered. Temptation was vying with common sense. 'It's… Well… Are you sure?'

'I offered,' he pointed out. 'I only have one condition.'

'Condition?'

He smiled, and that delicious curl of his mouth, which made her chest leap and burst like popcorn in a microwave, made Effie narrow her eyes.

She told herself it was nerves that she felt and not anticipation that coursed through her.

His mouth curled up even more sinfully. 'I need you to come on another date with me.'

Pins and needles scattered through her body. Heat and cold. Dark and light. Exhilaration and fear.

It didn't matter how long she might stay there, scanning his face and trying to analyse what was going on in his mind, he was too closed-off, too controlled.

'A date?'

'Yes. You know—two people getting together for a social activity where romance is a distinct possibility.'

She frowned. 'Or, in our case, the pretence of romance?'

He paused, and for one glorious moment she thought he was going to deny it.

'Of course,' he confirmed, and something darted over his features, too fast for Effie to work out what it was.

Probably relief. Which, she told himself, was just fine.

'I thought we might go to a restaurant frequented by some contacts of my parents. News of our date—and no doubt the odd phone photo—will have made its way across two continents before Chef Michel's world-renowned soufflé can even be served.'

'I thought that was what our gala date was supposed to have been about?'

'It was.'

He shrugged, as though he wasn't remotely affected by this conversation. And, of course, she reminded herself hastily, neither was she.

'But that was a work thing. This is a private date. It will consolidate the image of us as a proper couple.'

A proper couple. The notion affected her exactly the way it shouldn't have done. Yet somehow she managed a curt nod. As one might acknowledge a point of fact in the operating theatre. Or the boardroom.

And it *wasn't* disillusionment which rumbled through her. Of course it wasn't.

The restaurant was excruciatingly romantic.

Intimate tables for two were dotted under a starry sky in one of the most booked-out restaurants in the city. Exactly as he'd planned. A place to see and be seen, just as he wanted. A set-up guaranteeing that word would get back to anyone in his family who hoped they could use him in a marriage arranged only to further their own agendas.

And yet all Tak wanted to do was lift Effie out of her chair and get out of there. To somewhere far more discreetly intimate. Where it would be just the two of them.

He fought to tune out the loved-up diners around them and concentrate instead as Effie chatted to him conversationally. He hadn't brought her here tonight to seduce her, or to further any romantic entanglement, so why was it that all he could think was that he wanted to taste her lips again, the way he had the night of the hospital gala?

'So *that's* what brought Nell and I halfway across the country,' Effie concluded.

He let his eyes linger a little too long on her mouth, fighting the impulse to lean right across the table and scoop her up, settle her on his knee and lick every inch of that smooth, elegant neck with his tongue. To hell with all the people, all the camera phones around them.

'That's a fascinating but I fear highly diluted story of what brought you to the air ambulance.' He hadn't intended his voice to sound so raw, so raspy, but she had him on edge tonight. Even more than usual.

Effie flushed, sucking in her bottom lip in a way that shot right through his body.

'I don't know what you mean,' she said.

'I think you do. You haven't really told me a single thing about you.' He had no idea why it even mattered, and yet the words kept coming. 'My few questions about your childhood were met with a wave and a comment that it was just like everyone else's—fairly standard. When I enquired after your family you smiled prettily and pointed out that in a job like ours we're so busy we never get to see people as much as we would like.'

'I don't see what's wrong with that.' She leaned back in her chair defensively.

'They weren't particularly intrusive questions, Effie. Just the usual kind of questions when two people are getting to know each other on a date.'

'Well…' She shrugged awkwardly, as though looking for an excuse, babbled on as soon as she thought she'd found one. 'Well, this isn't a date, is it? You said it yourself—it's just shoring up the falsehood of our being in a relationship to distract your extended family from pushing the idea of an arranged marriage.'

Yes, he *had* said that, hadn't he? Tak clenched his fist, unseen. The problem was, even at the time he had known that wasn't true. Even in that moment when he'd asked her on a date a part of him had known that it was because he'd genuinely wanted to take her out.

Fooling his extended family was merely an added bonus, a justification. Though whether for Effie's benefit or for his own, he couldn't be sure.

And so all through the meal he'd felt his frustration growing as she fed him her all too practised response, telling him the carefully crafted version of her life that she wanted him to hear.

Nothing more, nothing less. Certainly not the truth. Nothing that would help him to understand the real Effie.

And he realised with a jolt that he *wanted* to know the real Effie. More than that, he *needed* to know the real Effie. Even if he couldn't understand why any more than he could understand why, as he'd listened to her prepared formulaic story, he'd let her soft, lilting voice distract him into imagining that mouth doing so many other things. Imagining her in his bed. As though he was some kind of hormone-ravaged teenager.

It was galling. He didn't *want* to want her, and yet since she'd swept into his life he'd felt as though everything he'd carefully built up around himself had been knocked down. And the solid foundations he'd thought he'd put down were now shown up for little more than wet sand.

From the instant Hetti had thrown Effie into his path as his plus one he'd been entranced. He could dress it up any way he wanted, label it with any number of excuses, but the unavoidable truth was that Effie made him hard, and greedy, and savage. And he wanted her with an intensity that was almost suffocating.

All the things his father had claimed to feel

about every one of his mistresses when he had rubbed them in the face of Tak's mother. The old man had never shown an ounce of respect for his wife or for his children. And he hadn't had a shred of self-control over his own vices. His father had been selfish right to his very core.

Fury and self-disgust flooded Tak's body. He'd spent his entire life trying not to be like his father—*ensuring* he wouldn't be like him by avoiding any kind of serious relationship. Which wasn't to say he hadn't enjoyed casual relationships… girlfriends lasting a few months…good sex.

But nothing had come even remotely close to this…*hunger* gnawing inside him ever since Effie Robinson had walked into his life. He wanted her. In the most primal way that a man could want a woman. He *wanted* her. *Only* her. And he couldn't pretend otherwise any longer.

'Why did you agree to accompany me to the hospital ball that night, Effie?' His voice was harsh, commanding, yet he still couldn't read the expression which flitted across her face.

'You know why. This is a new place for me… there are men who view my single status as a challenge, and I have a daughter who is the sole focus of my life. Fake dating you was the quickest way to make anyone else back off, and when we "break up" I get to pretend that I'm not dating because I'm not over you.'

'You have it all worked out, don't you?' He ran

a finger around the rim of his wine glass, if only to stop himself from reaching over the table and touching her.

'As much as you do,' Effie hedged, with that inscrutable darkness shadowing her eyes again.

'Except that you've made me curious about you. I want to know why you're so untrusting of people. Of men.'

'It isn't just about men,' she answered—too quickly, not realising she was giving herself away until it was too late.

There was no reason for it to feel like such a victory. And yet he leapt on it all the same. 'Everyone, then. Why?'

'That isn't what I meant.' She flushed crossly.

'It isn't what you meant to *say*, no. But it *is* what you meant. Deep down.'

'I thought tonight was about giving a convincing show?' she bit out. 'Not about delving into areas of each other's lives which are best left unexplored.'

It had been. Only he'd changed the rules. Unfairly, perhaps, but he hadn't been able to help himself. It seemed his usual sense of boundaries was slipping, sliding away from him. Certainly where Effie was concerned.

Why would he have offered to take Nell to that party if not because he wanted to make Effie happy? To show him she needed him?

Why?

The realisation hit him hard and low, and something gathered inside him, gaining momentum, and power, and a voice. So loud that it howled inside him with all the truths that it brought.

It was one thing to want Effie physically. Sexually. But it was quite another to sit here, in this restaurant, in the middle of this *performance*, and realise that he wanted more. That he wanted her on an emotional level, too.

He wanted to know about her life and her family, about what had happened to mould her and shape her, about every single event which had led up to her and her daughter living in that awful flat in that awful building.

He wanted to know her, *truly* know her, and to understand her. And he wanted to tell her all the things he'd never been able to tell anyone in his life before. Not even Hetti.

The urge was almost overwhelming. He even opened his mouth to speak. But nothing came out. An internal struggle was going on inside him and it was as though he was floating outside his own body, able only to watch. Never to intervene.

Somehow he managed to rein himself back in. Curb himself. Stifle this insane compulsion which had come out of nowhere.

But it cost him. He couldn't talk to Effie. Not about any of it. He would never be able to do that. Because if he did then it would mean he was putting his own selfish desires ahead of what he knew to be best for others. Just like his father had done.

He knew the pattern. He'd seen it so many times before, and each time he'd watched it rip out another little piece of his mother's soul.

Once this initial fervour wore off—and whether that was in a month, six months, a year, much as it felt impossible now, he knew it would happen, it was inexorable, just as his father had always said—he would end up letting Effie down. Hurting her. Betraying her.

Yes, he knew the pattern. He'd just never imagined he'd be the one copying it. It was madness and it had to stop.

He had to stop it. *Now*.

'Are you all right?'

Effie peered at Tak and tried to control her racing heart. The entire evening had been unsettling, from the fancy restaurant to Tak's too-close-to-home questions. In all her life she had never found it so hard to recite her practised lies. Never before had she felt such a desperate yearning to throw away her mask and finally let somebody see the real Effie.

But what if Tak hated that person? What if he hated the mess, the ugliness that was her past? And it was so very, *very* ugly. There was no dressing it up and passing it off as something palatable.

An ache pooled deep in her belly as she

watched Tak through lowered lashes. He looked more incredible than ever tonight, in that sleek, smart-casual suit. A lesson in sheer male perfection—all hard lines and intriguing shadows. Solid and utterly, devastatingly imposing.

And he was all *hers*.

At least he was pretending to be.

And that was the irony of it, wasn't it? They were out in public so that they could fool other people, but the person most at risk of falling for the charade was herself.

'I'm quite well, thank you.'

His rich voice glided over her skin like silk.

'Did you imagine otherwise?'

'You seem…distracted,' she offered, before correcting herself. 'On edge.'

'On the contrary, I'm feeling very much at ease in your company.'

It wasn't so much the way he said it—in that throwaway style of his, as though it was an easy compliment but didn't mean very much at all. It was more the way his eyes darkened sinfully, possessively, almost as though against his will.

Her pulse beat out a thrilled tattoo. She could feel it thrumming in her neck. And she could feel it thrumming somewhere altogether more intimate.

Everywhere Tak went people turned their heads to watch him, to admire him. He inspired admiration and envy alike, and his renowned career made him a man to hold in the highest esteem.

But when he looked at her like that he made Effie feel as though she was the only thing in the world that he saw. The only woman he would ever want. And when he laughed it was as if he'd shot her through with a thousand bright volts. It was heady, and intoxicating, and utterly, completely dangerous.

Because it made her forget that this was all simply a game.

'So, what's the plan? We've been here an hour already. Do you think the news will have got back to your family, or do we need to do something more memorable?'

'More memorable?' he arched an eyebrow. 'What, exactly?'

'I don't know!' Effie chuckled, for no obvious reason but that he made her feel happy. 'Maybe... Well, perhaps... Hmm...

'Causing a scene about the food before sending it back?' he speculated, making Effie gasp.

'No. That would be horrible! The staff—goodness the chef!'

'Why doesn't that surprise me? I imagine you're the kind of person who smiles and says the meal is lovely even if it truly is ghastly.'

She knew she looked sheepish. She certainly felt sheepish. 'I suppose that is what I do,' she conceded. 'Not that I dine out often, that is.'

'Perhaps we should do something about that.' He laughed, and then, before she could ask him what he'd meant by that, he changed the subject. 'So, if not memorable that way, then how?'

It made no sense that her heart should be beating so hard. And this time when she smiled it didn't feel quite so easy. 'I don't know. Forget I said anything.'

'Do you suppose I should stand up and come around the table? Haul you into my arms before kissing you? Not a light peck, you understand, but a thorough, unmistakable kiss, designed to conquer rather than simply confide.'

'No!' she denied, even though every fibre of her was screaming that she was lying. 'Of course that isn't what I was saying.'

And then she swallowed. Hard. It was a fatal mistake.

Tak's eyes snapped to her throat, then locked onto her gaze, and it was as though she was laid bare and he could read every inch of her soul. Could appreciate every last one of her darkest desires.

All of which seemed to centre around him.

'You *do* want me to do that,' he declared, and she might have believed that he had not truly thought so before. That a part of him even welcomed the revelation.

But then his expression turned hard, cold. 'I was given to understand that you don't want a relationship with anyone. It was one of the reasons I agreed to take you to the ball as my plus one.'

She felt as if he had stamped his foot into her chest and crushed it down. Later, when she actually thought about it, she still wouldn't understand how she didn't crumple with shame right there in front of him.

'You *invited* me as your date to the ball because it was mutually convenient. We were each other's buffers and we played our roles to perfection.'

'Yet now here you are...wanting more.'

She could feel the heat spreading across her neck, her cheeks, but she lifted her head and refused to be intimidated. 'I have never suggested I want more. *You* are the one who insisted Nell and I couldn't stay in our flat. *You* are the one who was so quick to open your door to us. And *you* are the one who has been interrogating me about my past and my family all evening. Almost as though you're interested. Perhaps I might suggest that this unexpected talk of kissing is more a reflection of *your* state of mind than mine.'

It had been a ruse. An attempt to bat the proverbial ball back into his court. Effie certainly hadn't expected her words to elicit any reaction— and certainly not one that suggested her words might not be as fantastical as she had thought them to be.

She watched, fascinated, as he scowled, and his eyes glittered almost black as he sat unnaturally still—rigid, even—in his seat. Her words had hit a target she hadn't even known existed.

'I'm right…' she breathed, almost in awe. 'You want me.'

His mouth flattened, and his glower was enough to intimidate even the boldest of women, but Effie stood her ground even as the blood roared in her ears.

And then, unexpectedly, the frown cleared and he eyed her in a way which was far more threatening—for it was pure desire and unrestrained hunger.

'You're right. I do want you,' he murmured at length. 'Just as you want me.'

She opened her mouth to deny it again, then snapped it shut. What was the point in lying? She didn't even know who she'd be lying to most. Tak or herself.

'Therefore why not embrace it? Use it to our advantage?'

'Use it?' she echoed, not following.

'Use this sexual attraction, this chemistry…'

His mouth curled into something so spectacularly sinful that she could feel the heat blooming through her very core.

'And fool everyone into thinking there is something really serious between us.'

'You mean, pretend…*more*?' she asked.

'I mean, pretend less,' he growled.

It took her a moment before the full implication of what Tak meant hit home.

Effie gasped. 'You mean, give in to this...this physical *thing* between us?' Her voice sounded too raw, too naked. 'Indulge? Have...have sex, or whatever, and let the rest of the world draw their own conclusions?'

'I'm curious,' he said almost idly. 'What's the *whatever*?'

She shook her head, confused. 'Pardon?'

'You said, *"have...sex, or whatever"*. I want to know what the *whatever* is? It sounds deliciously naughty.'

His lips curved licentiously and he made no attempt to hide his amusement. Effie's entire body trembled—and not, she feared, with disgust.

'You're being deliberately provocative,' she accused shakily.

'Is that a problem?'

'It's...aggravating.'

'Is that so?' Tak demurred. 'Any time you think I have it wrong, be sure to let me know and I shall stop at once.'

And there it was. The way to put this entire evening back twenty-four hours, to make it clear that she wasn't interested in anything other than a pretend show. All she had to do was tell him he was wrong.

Instead, she deflected. 'This all started because

I asked you if you needed a scene to ensure word of our date got back to your family.'

'I remember,' he agreed, a little too knowingly. 'And *I* asked if you meant me to kiss you.'

'I told you I didn't.'

'Which I believe we've already established was a lie. We appear to be going around in circles, *priya*.' Abruptly he stood up, dark and intent. 'Allow me to break the cycle.'

She knew what he was doing even before he moved around the table. She ought to say something. She had to stop him. Instead she raised her hands slightly to meet his as he drew her out of her seat.

And then she was pressed against his body. Soft heat against inflexible steel. White-hot explosions in her body competed with the thrilling fireworks in her head. She was like a coiled spring, held under tension, and it was all the more unbearable as Tak lowered his mouth to hers and held it there. Refusing to close that gap completely. The heat of his breath on her lips was driving her delirious with longing.

'Do you think they've had a good enough show?' he pondered.

'Hmm…?'

'The other diners. Will they have their phones out yet?'

She might have been insulted, but she heard the

crack in his voice and knew he was only holding on by the skin of his teeth.

'Good point.' She stopped, as though to consider, although it nearly killed her. 'A little longer, I think.'

Her reward was a rumble of disapproval from Tak before he lowered his head to claim her lips.

The kiss was every bit as electrifying as their first one outside her apartment door. Had it only been ten days ago? It felt like a lifetime. Or a life sentence. Perhaps because she'd been waiting her entire life for a kiss like this. For a man like this.

She forgot completely where they were, or the game they had been playing. All she knew was Tak, and the way he was kissing her. She was drowning in him all over again, pouring herself into him as she moulded every inch of her body to his.

All that subtle flirting, all those heady glances, all that repressed desire was unleashed in this single moment. As though it would never end.

He plundered her mouth, demanding and devouring with every scandalous swipe of his tongue and every luscious graze of his teeth. And Effie was all too happy to lose herself in the lustiness of it all.

Right up until the moment he moved his hands to her shoulders and pushed her back.

'I cannot do this,' he ground out, his face twisted into something she didn't recognise.

'Tak…'

'I cannot do this,' he repeated quietly. Obdurately. 'With you, least of all.'

Effie was wholly unprepared for the pain as the words sliced through her. A lifetime of being told, directly or indirectly, that she wasn't good enough—that *she* wasn't enough—flooded through her. Hateful and merciless. She'd thought she'd buried her past a long, long time ago. Yet one utterance from Tak and instantly she felt like that pathetic, rejected girl she'd never really left behind.

Grief blinded her, but she knew the one thing she couldn't afford to do was let Tak see it.

With Herculean resolve, Effie turned slowly and forced herself to take her time picking up her clutch. She would not run out of here. She would not turn and flee with her tail between her legs like some unwanted, abandoned puppy.

'Well, then…' She cleared her throat, amazed at how collected she'd managed to sound. 'That settles that debate, doesn't it?'

And she turned and stalked off, head held high, out of the restaurant and into a parked taxi before Tak had even moved a muscle.

Her tears could wait until she was alone. The way they always had.

CHAPTER NINE

'THAT SOUNDS LIKE an emphatic crack,' Tak approved, as he carefully lifted out a section of his patient's skull and began to clear away the dura to expose her brain. 'Okay, we have good access to the temporal lobe now, and the tumour is hiding in there. Time to map her brain, so go ahead and wake her up.'

He waited as his co-pilot and the anaesthetist worked together to bring the patient to the level of awareness he would need her to have in order to carry out his language tests as he passed a series of electrical currents over her brain to map it.

The lull was unwelcome. It created a void in the operation and allowed his own brain the chance to reflect on things he would rather not have to mull over.

Like the way everything had changed when he'd touched Effie, held her, kissed her last night.

One minute they'd been playing some kind of game, and the next he had completely taken leave of his senses. Felt the same kind of madness taking hold of him that he had always despised in his selfish, ruthless father. The man who had taken such delight in telling his wife time and again that his latest mistress made him feel alive in a way that Tak's mother never could.

The same kind of selfishness that Rafi had shown, taking a mistress of his own and believing it was perfectly normal even though he'd seen how it had devastated their mother. Worse, Rafi had said contemptuously that Uma Basu—he hadn't called her Mama since he'd turned fifteen—was foolish, emotional, even irrational. That her depressions and addictions were of her own making, and even that they excused their father for needing to find companionship elsewhere, rather than it being his father's actions causing Uma's devastation.

Tak couldn't say he thought his brother was entirely wrong—their mother *was* quite the master manipulator—though what had come first, her machinations or his father's cruelty, was a question he couldn't answer.

Either way, he'd spent his whole life avoiding being like either his father or his brother. He'd thought he'd succeeded. His relationships had always been fine. He had sated his physical and emotional desires without ever feeling as though he wasn't in control.

Until last night. Or, more accurately, until Effie.

He could no longer deny the attraction which had been evident between them since that first meeting. Or the fact that he'd been acting irrationally since the hospital gala—not least when he'd commanded her to pack her bags and move herself and her daughter into his home.

He could couch it in whatever terms he liked—
Effie needing somewhere to live or him wanting
to distract his mother from her obsession with
arranging a marriage for him—but ultimately it
all came down to the fact that he'd wanted an excuse to spend more time with Effie. To indulge
this attraction which had slid so insidiously into
his entire body.

'Madeleine, can you hear me?'

As the neurologist dropped down behind the
sheets Tak switched quickly back to the task in
hand.

'Can you open your eyes for me, Madeleine?
Good. Now, can you stick out your tongue for
me?'

Working quickly and efficiently, Tak moved the
electric current over different areas of his patient's
brain. As the tests went on, through actions and
various language tests, he could work out which
parts of Madeleine's brain were responsible for
key activities and try to avoid these areas when
he moved in to try to remove the tumour.

They were partway through the first series of
exercises, the reciting of the alphabet, when the
neurologist signalled to him to slow down.

'Okay, Tak.' Her voice carried low but clear.
'We have some problems in this area.'

'Understood.' Tak nodded to his colleague.

It seemed as though they were near a vital
speech area of Madeleine's brain, from where he

would be unable to remove the tumour. But they were only a short while into the operation and their patient was already becoming increasingly tired, finding it harder and harder to stay awake.

He had ideally anticipated three hours' brain-mapping for this size tumour, but they were barely ninety minutes in. If they didn't work quickly Tak risked missing out on the vital brain-mapping information that would enable him to remove the tumour without compromising their patient's brain function.

It was the kind of challenge which spurred him on—even more so today, when he didn't want to think about anything but his work.

If only everything in his life could be pigeon-holed so damned easily.

For several almost blissful hours Tak concentrated on his surgery.

And the next. And the next.

Yet the minute he was out of the operating room, and his shift was over, his brain was flooded afresh with images of Effie. They had been becoming more and more insistent all week. Ever since he'd taken Effie on that disastrous date, since he'd taken Effie's daughter to that bowling alley.

He had no idea what it was about Effie—about wanting to make the woman happy—that had possessed him to volunteer to chaperone her kid at a party. Not that it had been a chore. The girl had chattered non-stop, even whilst climbing into his sleek, muscular super-car. Undisguised happiness had danced off her every word, and as far as she was concerned the evening had been a resounding success.

Just as undisguised happiness had danced around in *him* at the idea that he was doing something for Effie, making her life a little easier.

Nell had been happy. Which meant that Effie was happy. Because her happiness was intrinsically linked with that of her daughter. It was sweet.

When the hell had he ever cared about anything *sweet*? But it mattered to him. *She* mattered. Yet he had no explanation for why. He didn't even stop to consider it. Deliberately.

He didn't want to dig into his emotions or responses. He didn't wish to ask himself why he had practically jumped at the chance to insert himself deeper into Effie's family life. He hadn't allowed himself to ask any one of the hundreds of questions which charged around his head.

He told himself that the only reason he'd insisted they stayed with him was because it would have been inhumane to knowingly leave mother and daughter in that freezing flat. He refused to acknowledge that it had anything to do with the kick which had reverberated around his body that first time he'd seen her stride into Resus. Or the fire which had ripped through him when he'd walked into that lobby to see her standing there so regally. Not to mention the passion that had later flared between them on that restaurant date.

It made no sense. Perhaps it was because he knew that soon Effie would be gone and life would revert back to normal.

The knowledge should please him. Not make him feel as though a weight was pressing down inside his chest.

It was the familiarity of it all, he concluded eventually. It was simply that he was drawing parallels between Effie's life, caring for her only just teenage daughter, with *his* life growing up, when he had often had sole responsibility for his younger teenage siblings, Hetti and Sasha. And Rafi too, for that matter, although he'd barely been nine at that time.

He remembered those feelings of loneliness and being scared, especially when his mother had been going through one of her episodes.

But wasn't that part of the issue? He and Effie had agreed to be each other's buffers. Nothing more. She wasn't supposed to be making him take trips down memory lane. He certainly wasn't supposed to be playing at happy families and helping out with her daughter.

Was he somehow giving her the impression that there was something between them? Playing with Effie's emotions in much the same way that his father had always so cruelly toyed with his mother's feelings? Surely it was a case of *like father like son*. Rafi had definitely suggested that was the case with his own wife.'

'I'm not our father,' Tak growled to himself, but the accusation pounded through him, making the blood heat in his veins.

Abruptly he realised he was outside the hospital and at his car, with no memory of how he'd even got there. He hit the ignition button, revved the engine, and pulled neatly out of the parking bay and onto the road beyond. He'd go for a drive. A long, fast drive in his prized car—the kind of vehicle which wasn't at all conducive to a man with a wife and kids. It would clear his head and remind him of exactly what he wanted his life to look like.

And it wasn't settling down. Because what if he was wrong? What if he *was* like his father, much as it might gall him? If there was any chance he was like that man, then Tak knew he would inevitably hurt his family, exactly the way his own father had hurt his.

Which was why he couldn't go home. Not with Effie and Nell there. Reminding him of the family he could never have. That life wasn't for him, and the sooner he remembered that, the better.

It was the early hours of the morning when Tak returned home, his head finally clear. Or at least as clear as it was going to get.

He still hadn't solved the puzzle that was Dr Effie Robinson, or why she so intrigued him. But he *had* convinced himself that he didn't have time for riddles and games.

Their original agreement—to play each other's buffer at the hospital gala—had worked perfectly. The rest of it was unnecessary complications which they should have avoided. That date at the restaurant should have been avoided. The kisses certainly should have been avoided.

But the beauty of it was that as soon as the central heating was fixed in Effie's flat and the asbestos was gone, *she* would be gone. And he could pretend all this had never happened.

In the meantime, sleep was certainly going to elude him.

Tak wandered down to the games suite.

The last person he'd expected to see there was Effie. And he certainly hadn't expected to see her, cue in hand, making the perfect pool game break, as though she was some kind of hustler.

He stopped, ridiculously enchanted all over again. Just like that.

It was only when he watched her pot the final black that he realised he'd watched her play an entire game. Lurking in the shadows like some kind of admirer from afar. Like some kind of adolescent kid.

'I didn't know you played,' he said, stepping out into the room.

She jumped, as if he'd caught her red-handed.

He made a mental note to get the lighting in the room changed. It had been designed to be ambient, but right now he didn't like the way the soft glow bounced off the walls, making the place feel so cosy, so…intimate. Yet ironically making him feel just that little bit too exposed.

He could put it down to the time of night—*bewitched at the witching hour.* But that suggested a ridiculous fancifulness with which he wasn't commonly associated.

'I don't play nowadays, but that doesn't mean I can't play.'

'So I've just witnessed. Misspent youth?' He quirked an eyebrow.

'You could say that.'

Her tone was casual. Perhaps too casual.

'Sounds intriguing.'

'It isn't,' she bit out, and he hated it that there was such a divide between them now. Especially when he knew he was the one who had created it, with that kiss the other night.

He should walk away. But not for the first time he stayed still instead. 'I owe you an apology.'

She grimaced.

'I should not have kissed you the other night. Perhaps I shouldn't have even taken you there.'

It was as if a hurricane was raging around them, but in the eye of it there was simply stillness. A hush.

'You didn't force my hand,' she said at length, gritting her teeth. 'And at least I now know where we stand. What you really think of me.'

'What I really think of you?' He frowned, but she merely turned away.

Clearly Effie didn't want to elaborate, and he tried to convince himself that he didn't care. This was exactly what he'd spent the last few hours repeating to himself. *It...she...wasn't his business.* When it came to Effie there *wasn't* something clawing inside him, desperate to find its way out.

But, despite everything he'd thought during that exhilarating drive, nothing compared to this unexpected wallop of insatiable need. This urge to learn more about this surprisingly enigmatic woman, even as a part of him knew she would never tell him.

'Effie, I shouldn't have kissed you because of *my* reasons. Nothing to do with you. Not really.'

'Is this the old *it's not me, it's you?*' She turned on him instantly, her voice a little too bright, too high, too tight. 'Only I've heard that a hundred times before.'

He wasn't prepared for the jealousy which sliced through him.

'Is that why you reacted the way you did? And why you don't date? Because some idiot bloke— Nell's father, maybe—once used that cliché and hurt you?'

'You think this is about some *guy*?' She shook

her head incredulously. 'That I would carry around something so banal and frankly inconsequential for thirteen years?'

'Then *what*?'

She stared at him, and then suddenly she wasn't seeing him any more—she was staring right through him.

'What is it that I don't understand about you, Effie?' he asked softly. 'You're intelligent and driven and beautiful. You're career-minded and you have Nell—I know that—but why are you so insistent on doing everything alone? On making sure no one ever gets close? You get more than your fair share of male attention but you shut every bit of it down before you can even think about giving it a chance.'

She flattened her lips together, clearly not about to answer him. He knew if he pushed her she would only shut down all the faster.

'I'll leave you to your game,' he managed softly, turning around to leave. Pretending that, for all the difficult things he'd had to do in his life, walking away from Effie wasn't one of the hardest.

Whether it was the hour, or the quiet, or the windowless nature of the games den which made it feel as if they were totally disconnected from the rest of the world, he couldn't be sure. But he heard her as she carefully placed the pool cue down on the table.

CHAPTER TEN

TAK WAS ABOUT to leave again when Effie suddenly hunched her shoulders lightly and—incredibly—answered him. Even if it sounded as though her mouth was struggling to form every single syllable.

'I guess. Yes.'

He waited a little longer, not about to make the same mistake again by pushing her.

Still, it felt like an eternity before she rewarded him by elaborating, 'It was the way you didn't think twice about what would happen if you won all those lots. You could just…*pay*. I spent so many years worrying where my next meal came from—even before Nell came along.'

'You've done an incredible job,' he pointed out.

'I guess…'

Effie dipped her head slightly, and he was gratified that the words didn't sound quite as stiff and awkward now. Almost as if she was beginning to trust him.

'My flat might not be anything compared to this, but it's mine. At least I pay the rent. I keep a roof over my kid's head. I keep her warm and fed and happy, and I give her the things she needs. I suppose I felt as though coming here was an admission that I wasn't a good enough mother.'

'Tak, wait.'

He turned and came back down a couple of steps. Effie was staring at the rich burgundy baize and it took Herculean strength for him not to speak. He couldn't remember the last time he'd wanted to know something about a woman so badly. So desperately. But she had to open up to him voluntarily. If he pushed her then she was likely to shut down again.

For long moments the quiet swirled around them, like the soft artificial smoke rising on the stage in one of the shows he'd taken his mother to see during her visits.

Tak had a feeling they were the only times Mama had got to do something *she* liked for a change. Even now his father would never deign to give her an hour of his time for something he termed so *terminally dull*.

'I'm sorry.' Effie seemed to brace herself. 'It's more about my childhood than some stupid lad—it wasn't exactly conventional. Anyway, it was wrong of me to take it out on you.'

She was trying to relegate her outburst to the past. But he wasn't about to let her. It was the closest he'd come to seeing the real Effie.

'What was so different about it?'

'Please, can we just leave it at that?'

'Is this why you don't talk about your family?'

'I don't *have* a family,' she burst out before checking herself.

Pursing her lips, she inhaled and exhaled heavily through her nose. And still he held himself still. Silent.

'I had a mother—some of the time—but I spent a lot of time in and out of children's homes and foster families.'

'You were a foster kid?'

'On and off. Not enough to be given a family of my own, but enough that I spent most of my childhood shunted in and out of other people's homes. I grew up resenting everything. Not least the fact that my mother couldn't get herself together enough to keep me safe whilst other kids were complaining that their mums had given them cheese sandwiches for lunch again when they'd wanted ham.'

If she'd punched him in the guts he couldn't have felt any more winded. Effie had been a foster kid? She was so not what he might have expected of one. Although now he thought about it he had no idea what that might have been.

He was only grateful that she continued.

'You know one of the worst things about it? You always feel like you're nothing and no one. And the older you get, the fewer families want you. Because they think you're going to give them attitude. And maybe it's true. But that's only because you're always made to feel like you should show more gratitude.'

'Gratitude?'

'Yes. And I *was* grateful—inside. But I also hated the fact that this was my life, so it was hard to be grateful when you saw what other kids—normal kids—got. So many foster families acted as though I should be doing cartwheels up and down the street in gratitude for a safe place to sleep, a warm bed, food on the table. It just reminded me of how different I was, because those were things that normal kids wouldn't even think twice about.'

'Is that why you were so resistant to take up my offer to come here?' he asked quietly, unable to help himself. 'Why you balked at my spending all that money at the silent auction?'

As her jaw set, her eyes going a steely grey as though she was shutting down, he mentally kicked himself for allowing the words to come out of his mouth. She was going to pull even further away from him now. The knowledge saddened him far more than it had any right to do.

'That boiler breaking down and your crappy landlord are no reflection on your ability as a mother.'

'But they *are*.' She lifted her head finally to meet his gaze and Tak stepped down the last couple of steps. 'At least they feel as though they are. If I could afford somewhere better, a house of our own, I wouldn't have to rely on some landlord. Or even if I could afford a better apartment closer to the helicopter base. Or even a car I could rely on if I lived further out.'

'Effie, you've raised a child from the age of eighteen and managed to get through medical school—and not just at *any* university, but one of the top places in the world—as well as forge a career as a trauma doctor. You've proved yourself a good mother over and over again.'

'And yet you've just walked in and seen me playing pool and I feel like a teenage kid caught red-handed again.'

Red-handed? Tak frowned. 'You weren't allowed to go to youth club and shoot pool when you were a kid?'

'It wasn't a youth club.'

A red stain crept over her skin and yet she kept talking to him. It suddenly occurred to him that this was Effie trusting him.

'It was an adult snooker hall. When things were bad at home, or a foster home, it was sometimes better to be elsewhere. It was safer—and warmer—than a park bench.'

'You slept on a park bench?'

'A few times,' she shrugged, and he wondered what that meant.

Once? Five times? Twenty?

'One night I realised I could sneak into the club and hang out in the warmth until at least two in the morning when it closed.'

'How old were you?'

'At that time? I guess about thirteen. The same age that Nell is now.'

Tak's fists clenched, and it was all he could do not to identify the emotion which charged through him in that moment. 'And no one noticed you?'

'The owner did.'

She shrugged, as though it was no big deal. As though she didn't feel any of the anger which constricted his chest, choking off his ability to breathe with ease. He couldn't have spoken if he'd wanted to. All he could do was listen and wonder why it rattled him so much. Why *this woman's* past got under his skin as it did.

'But she turned a blind eye at first—except for warning some of the guys that if they went near me she'd kill them. Then, when my mum started going through her bad spells, and they became more frequent than not, she put a couch in a back office with what she called "leftovers".

She said it was hers, but that I could use it if she wasn't in there.'

'Let me guess—she only put it there for you to use?' His smile was bittersweet.

The woman's kindness was touching, but the fact that Effie's childhood had necessitated it was saddening. But for the circumstance of money they had both suffered because of weak mothers. How easily could this have been *his* life or his life been Effie's?

'Right.' Effie lifted her head a little, as if she was making a point of not letting her memories pull her back under. 'We both knew what she was doing, but neither of us ever said it aloud.'

'So she was the one person who didn't make you feel like you had to do cartwheels?'

'Pretty much.'

Her voice sounded thicker. Clogged. He wanted to know more but he didn't want to put her through it.

'How long did that go on for?'

'Every time my mother went through a bad patch I would go there, and Eleanor would see to it that I had food, clean clothes, a warm bed. Then, as the years went on, we began to talk—until eventually she gave me a key to her house and I could sneak in whenever things got bad at home.'

'She wasn't a foster parent, though?'

'No, but she was the closest thing to a mother

I've ever had. She was the one who saw I was bright but that I'd slipped behind because of my circumstances. She worked with me—even got on to one of the snooker players whose day job was a teacher to come and give me some private tuition. She paid him by giving him a year's annual pass.'

'She got you to believe in yourself?' Tak realised.

'Yes. I'd always dreamed of being a doctor—God knows where *that* came from—but she was the one who convinced me I could get into Oxford.'

'So what happened?' The need to understand burned so impossibly hot inside him. 'Did she get mad about you getting pregnant with Nell?'

He felt something shifted in an instant. He couldn't shake the fear that Effie was about to shut down again. Thrust him away. But slowly, eventually, she lifted her gaze to his.

'She never knew about Nell, Tak. Eleanor died two days after she'd received confirmation that she could officially adopt me. I went off the rails for a few months. I mean I *really* went all out. Which is when I fell pregnant.'

The cruelty of it slammed into him with a truly brutal force. He opened his mouth to speak but nothing came out. What words existed?

'Eleanor was the first person who'd ever made me feel wanted. Cared for. Loved.'

She shrugged. as though it was no big deal. and all of a sudden Tak appreciated the enormity of the weight Effie had been carrying around with her all these years. He understood why she didn't want anyone in her life. Why she felt as though she had to protect herself from any more heartbreak or rejection.

He wasn't even aware of closing the gap between them but suddenly there she was, in his arms, looking at him with a curious expression. He tried to make himself let go but it was impossible. Her inexplicable hold over him wouldn't allow it.

Effie watched, so still he didn't think she was even breathing. Her eyes locked with his, as though she was searching for answers he didn't want to give her, and he tried to block her out, stop her from seeing the truth. Stop her from realising just how desperately he wanted her.

He made to move away from her just as she twisted towards him. The contact rocketed through them both.

As her eyes widened with understanding Tak froze, very much afraid he was about lose his infamous control all over again. And that couldn't happen. Whatever the attraction between the two of them, he certainly couldn't give her what she needed. Hell, he would only detonate every rejection and insecurity she had ever had.

He dropped his arms, though it cost him dearly

to do so. 'I'm sorry,' he said again, but this time he injected it with every ounce of the regret and empathy he felt after hearing her story. As though he thought an apology for his own actions could somehow make it up to her for all the people in her life who should have apologised to her but hadn't.

'Why are you sorry?'

The sweet, soft smile which curled her lips might as well have plunged into his heart and twisted it into a knot.

'My past isn't your problem.'

'Then I'm sorry for those kisses.'

'Sorry you kissed me?' she challenged. 'Or sorry you stopped?'

'Don't do this, Effie,' he bit out.

His body felt supercharged, and he was all too aware that if he weakened, if he kissed her again, this time he might never stop.

'You actually meant it when you said it was more about you than about me.' It was a statement more than a question. A recognition.

'Effie…' It was a whisper carried on his hot breath.

She didn't heed the warning. Instead she smiled, and it wrecked him like nothing he could ever have imagined. Then she closed the gap and lifted her mouth to his, and as the blood roared in his head like a waterfall, or a drumbeat deep in his veins, pumping around his body, he gave himself up to the intensity of the kiss.

It was madness, but he couldn't bring himself to care…

There was no escaping it.

Not the kiss so much as the emotions which coursed through her as a result of it. And a heat so scorching it was almost white. Searing her from within and making her feel as if a thousand fires were all blazing inside her at once.

Everywhere.

Like nothing she'd ever known before.

And then Tak used one hand to cup her cheek almost tenderly, skimming the other hand down her body, his fingertips igniting every inch of her as it moved. She forgot every superfluous thought and merely revelled in the sublimity of his touch, his kiss, the way his eyes glittered with undisguised hunger.

He kissed her over and over, his tongue partnering hers in a sensual dance of their own, his teeth grazing her lips with just the perfect amount of pressure. He tilted his head for a better fit, a slicker fit. First one way and then the other, as if he needed to taste her thoroughly. Completely.

Effie had never felt so desired. Not that she knew how to show it, and she was all too aware of her inexperience, expecting Tak to be put off at any moment. But he wasn't. He just kept kissing her, holding her, helping her to relax with every delicious glide of his tongue. And all Effie could do was grip his shoulders—his strong, muscled shoulders, which only played even more havoc with her spinning, somersaulting insides—and hang on for the ride.

Abruptly Tak lifted her up, carrying her easily back to the snooker table and perching her on it. She wasn't sure what instinct made her wrap her legs around him, but there he was. The hardest part of him nestled against the softest part of her.

'Better…'

His thick-voiced murmur only sent her insides skittering all over again. She wasn't sure how she found a way to respond. 'Glad you approve.'

'Oh, you have no idea.'

His voice was like a hum, low and demanding, seeping through her flesh and reverberating around her body. And then he was slipping his T-shirt over his head, with hers following, and she could only savour the moment as he dipped his head and traced the line of her neck with his impossibly carnal tongue.

'Tak…' she breathed, scarcely recognising her own voice.

He didn't answer, instead dropping hot, sensual kisses behind her ear and into the oh-so-sensitive hollow by her throat.

Effie gave herself up to it. To every single, incredible sensation screaming through her body, telling her that this—*this*—was what she'd been missing all these years. The way her entire body seemed to melt against his, moulding itself to him as though it had been handcrafted just for Tak.

It felt like an age before he slid the thin strap of her bra down, his kisses blazing a trail over the creamy swell of her breast but stopping short and leaving her actually *aching* for more. She arched her back in silent objection and he actually managed a throaty chuckle. As if he liked teasing her this way.

If she was honest, she liked him teasing her this way, too. Especially when he unhooked her bra with a deft flick of his wrist and drew it from her, lowering his mouth to take its place, closing over her tight nipple with something approaching reverence.

Effie had no idea how long he stayed there, kissing and licking, his tongue swirling in intricate patterns, eliciting from her sounds which she'd never heard from herself before. He took his time, moving from one breast to the other and back again, unhurried and deliberate. An eternity of bliss.

She couldn't have moved or stopped him even if she'd tried. Even if she'd wanted to.

At some point she arched into him, pressing closer against his length. Hot and steely. Unmistakable. *For her.* A tantalising shiver racked her body.

And then he was stepping back, away from her.

Effie's eyes flew open. For a ghastly minute she thought he was leaving and her heart actually paused, like a trapeze artist flying through the air in that second before the audience knew whether she was going to be caught on the other side.

Before she could think, however, Tak lifted her up and carried her over to the couch. He laid her down with a sort of gentleness, before reaching for her jeans to unhook them and slide them off in a single, smooth movement.

The last scrap of lace followed and then she was naked. She might have expected to feel awkward or flustered, but Tak's hooded expression stopped her from throwing her arms across her chest and instead lent her an air of unanticipated confidence.

'Stunning,' he breathed, his eyes raking over her body just as effectively as if they were his hands.

'Now it's your turn,' she said, and there was a hoarse pitch to her voice.

He stepped towards her, then stopped himself. 'Are you on the pill?'

'Sorry?' The question jarred her.

'The pill?' he pressed, his urgency offering her a crumb of relief.

She bit her lip, offering a curt shake of her head. How had that not even entered her head? 'No. I haven't needed it.'

'You haven't needed protection?' he frowned.

Her cheeks burned. 'No. Yes. It's just… I haven't… Not since Nell was conceived…'

If he was surprised, he hid it well. Closing the space between them again, he let his hands cradle either side of her face, dropping a long, deep kiss on her lips.

'Then we're just going to have to find a different way,' he murmured, setting tiny kisses at the corners of her mouth and back down her neckline.

As his hands moved over her body, slightly callused thumbs flickering expertly over the straining pink buds of her nipples, all other thoughts slid out of her head. And then his hand traced down her body from her long throat, over her breasts to her stomach, and finally to her aching core. He nestled his head between her thighs.

Effie froze. She wasn't completely naïve. She knew what he was about to do. But a part of her brain still couldn't process it. No one had ever done this to her before. Sex with Nell's father had been fumbled, missionary. Two kids who'd had no real idea what they were doing. Not like this. Not like *him*.

'Tak.' Her voice was tense even to her ears.

'Relax,' he soothed, kissing his way up the inside of one thigh. 'I've been dreaming about tasting you since the first moment I saw you.'

'Yes, but…'

'Relax,' he murmured again as he moved over

to the other thigh. His grin was nothing short of devilish.

'Tak, listen…'

And then he licked his way into her and a thousand fireworks went off in her head all at once. Long, slow strokes of his tongue were followed by darting little licks which had her lips moving entirely of their own volition, her hands reaching down to his hair. She slid her fingers into the thick depths, urging him on as if she couldn't help herself.

Frankly, she couldn't.

She wanted Tak so badly that it almost scared her.

And for his part he seemed to read her mind, knowing what she needed from him even before she knew it herself. His tongue was like a weapon, conquering her and inflaming her all at once, whipping her up until she felt she couldn't take any more. And then he eased back long enough for her to catch her breath before stoking her up all over again.

Effie was powerless to stop him. Not that she really wanted to. Beneath his mouth her hips rocked and lifted, as if she couldn't get enough of him—and perhaps she couldn't. Perhaps she never wanted this to end. But then he was driving her on, driving her upwards to where it was dazzling and spinning, and she knew there was no coming back from it this time.

And she broke apart. His mouth was still on her as she shattered around him, scarcely recognising the sounds coming from herself, only knowing that nothing would ever be the same again.

What the hell was he doing?

It took Tak a superhuman effort to stand up, away from Effie, but if he didn't then he wasn't sure he was going to be able to stop himself from claiming her as his—right there and then, protection be damned.

She was like no woman he'd ever been with before. Her taste was still in his mouth, her exquisite scent too, and all he could think was that he wanted more. He was greedy for her, *aching* for her. He wanted her completely.

But he couldn't let that happen. Sex was one thing. Emotions were something quite different. Yet, as impossible as it seemed, where Effie was concerned the two seemed wholly intertwined.

Incredibly, his legs were actually shaking as he made himself move away.

'Where are you going?'

Her low whisper halted him instantly. Evidence of her climax lingered in her tone, rushing straight to his sex as surely as if she'd taken hold of him.

'This was a...' he paused, unable to bring himself to say the word *mistake* '...an error of judgement.'

'Oh.'

A bright red stain covered her cheeks and neck, but he pretended not to notice as he located her clothes and passed them to her. He wanted to take it back. To tell Effie that she was the most incredible creature. He would never know how he held his tongue. He only knew that if he gave her any indication of how close he was to losing control—if she tested him in any way—he would fail. He wouldn't be able to resist her.

Such was her power over him. And the worst thing about it was that there was a part of him which silently urged Effie to do just that. Because failing to resist her would, at the end of the day, be a win.

Where was his damned T-shirt?

'We won't speak of this again,' he ground out, trying not to notice how she still sat on the couch, gloriously naked and making no attempt to conceal the soft curves which seemed to call every last inch of his body.

And then she shifted—stiffly, awkwardly, yanking her T-shirt on and concealing herself from him. Tak feared his resolve might crumble there and then. His only saving grace was that she clearly had no idea of the inexplicable hold she had over him.

To hell with his T-shirt. He needed to get out of there.

CHAPTER ELEVEN

WALKING INTO THE hospital to check on old Mrs Kemp—a woman she'd brought in on her last shift, who had no family—Effie was congratulating herself on having successfully avoided Tak for four days.

Yesterday's day off had been spent walking Nell to school, then spending the morning window shopping for things she couldn't afford. Anything to stay out of Tak's house. As huge as it was, it had felt small to her, knowing he was off too, that they could have spent the day together.

Today she'd come in to the hospital to see old Mrs Kemp and Tak was the last person she'd expected to see as she hurried on to the ward.

And he saw her instantly.

If only he'd been facing the other direction.

Unable to look away, or move, she simply stood there as he headed over, her throat dry. And Tak just walked closer and closer, until they were almost toe to toe. Not close enough to touch, but certainly enough that she could feel the warmth of his breath on her forehead. It was oddly intimate.

'You've been avoiding me.'

She could deny it. But he would know. And she didn't want to look even more pitiable than she already did. The shameful truth was that Tak's opinion of her had begun to matter. Which only made it all the more ludicrous that she should have opened herself up the other night, thereby confirming just how much of a charity case she really was.

'What were you doing, talking to Mrs Kemp?'

'And now you're changing the subject.'

His voice poured through her, altogether too liquid. 'I was merely asking a question,' she replied dryly, impressing even herself.

She might have known it wouldn't fool Tak.

'You were asking an *obvious* question,' he corrected. 'But, to answer, I'm here doing the same thing I imagine *you* are intending to do. Providing a bit of companionship to a lonely, frightened old woman.'

Something shouldered its way into her chest and lodged there. As hard as she tried, Effie couldn't ignore it. Was it sentiment at his show of compassion?

'And you came down here just for that?'

'*You* did,' he pointed out. 'She's asleep, by the way. Best not to disturb her.'

'You didn't really come to see her.' Effie was sceptical. 'How do you even *know* her?'

'You're the one who brought her in. How do you think?'

'They called you for a consult,' Effie acknowledged grudgingly. 'She told me she hadn't hit her head when she'd fallen but I suspected otherwise. She's okay?'

'Fine. But I'm also checking over a couple of other patients.' He quirked an all too astute eyebrow. 'Is that a more plausible reason for you? Or perhaps you were hoping that I was using Mrs Kemp as some sort of excuse to see if I could bump into you?'

Her cheeks were burning. She could feel the heat. Because the humiliating truth was that a small part of her possibly *did* wish there was an element of the latter to his visit. How pathetic did that make her?

Not for the first time, she wished she was the kind of person to whom witty retorts came easily. Instead she found her fuzzy brain scrambling for *anything* to say whilst it seemed more interested in the electrifying sensations that darted all over her body when Tak was near. Just as they had the other night.

She remembered barely getting to her room and slamming the door behind her before her legs had given out and she'd collapsed to the floor. She'd had no idea what had just happened. Or, more to the point, she'd known *what* had happened, she just hadn't understood how she'd let it happen. And with Tak Basu.

Forget the sex, she'd instructed herself as the familiar flush had soared through her. She would be able to over-analyse that particular turn of events later, and she certainly hadn't been ready to deal with that yet. What of the things she'd told Tak? Things she hadn't told a soul in almost fifteen years.

Eleanor Jarvis.

She'd hugged the name to herself like a favourite comforter. The woman after whom Effie's daughter had been named.

Eleanor. The woman who had seen her potential and convinced her to try for Oxford University, even though the kids in school had called her *thick* or *stinky* or a heck of a lot worse because she might not have been able to get home to have a shower for days. Even the teachers had let their distaste for her outward appearance blind them to the clever child she'd been underneath.

Eleanor. The woman who had been about to adopt her. To finally make Effie a part of something good. Something loving. Something special. Before a car crash had stolen Eleanor's life away. Hit by a drunk driver on her way home from the snooker hall one night.

And with that the driver had stolen away the last life-line at which Effie had been grasping. Gone. Snuffed out. In a single instant. Even now Effie still relived the pain, the loneliness, the suffocating blackness, whenever she thought about that night.

Which was why, the day after her daughter's birth, she'd made a point to banish those memo-

ries from her mind. Never to let herself go back.
Only to look forward.

That she should remember Eleanor at that moment, after Tak had…*done* things to her, had been
bad enough, but that she should have unravelled
so instantly at the memories had been so much
worse. Yet none of that had compared to the confused storm raging inside at the idea that, of all
people, Tak Basu, her colleague, should have been
the one to rake up all these memories.

She'd glanced at the clock. Six-thirty. Little
point in trying to go to sleep. Even though her
tiredness had gone bone-deep, she'd known sleep
would still elude her when her head was on that
pillow. Her head had been too full. Her brain too
feverish.

In the end she'd sneaked down to Tak's home
gym for a run, relieved to have the place to herself.

Unlike right now, when she couldn't seem to
get any privacy from him if her life depended
on it.

'You're very welcome to join me if you want,'
he offered.

As if he somehow knew that her life, aside
from Nell, was her career. Nothing more existed.
It hadn't for over a decade.

'Sorry.' She forced herself to sound jovial. 'I
have things to do. With Nell.'

'Yeah? Like what?'

Effie balked. *Think fast. Faster.*

She glanced up at the TV by the nearest bed. Some baking show. Perfect.

'We're making a cake,' she announced, before her brain had even had chance to get into gear.

'A cake?'

'Sure.' *Hell, why not?* 'Is there a problem with that?'

'Only that in all the time you've been staying at my home I haven't seen you cook once. I thought you didn't know how.'

'There's a huge difference between cooking and baking, you know,' Effie managed loftily.

'Indeed?'

Why did she get the impression that he was deliberately setting her up.

'What's that then?'

'Well...' She floundered. 'It's obvious, isn't it? Anyway, I have to go. Things to buy and all that.'

Before the shops closed and preferably before Nell decided to go out for the evening with a couple of friends. And if she could grab someone who actually knew the first thing about baking, then she would do that, too.

'Mum, you can't be serious! We're *not* spending a Saturday night baking fairy cakes together. I'm thirteen, not seven!'

Effie took it as a win that for all Nell's exclamations her daughter was still hovering at the door to the vast high-tech kitchen, as though a part of her wanted to come in.

'The flat will be ready soon, and then we'll be back home. I just wanted to do a personal thank-you to Hetti and Tak.'

'But a *cake*, Mum? You're not exactly the world's best baker.'

Which they both knew was an understatement. It was something Eleanor had promised to teach her. Before she'd died.

'What *else* are you going to do, Nell?'

It wasn't easy to make herself sound blasé. Not when a part of her was so desperate to find things to do—any time she found herself at a loose end—which were so family-orientated it would ensure she wasn't alone with Tak for the rest of their stay here.

Because he was right that what had happened between them the other night should never have transpired. Worse, since it *had* happened she hadn't been able to stop replaying it in her head. And even worse again was the fact that in her re-runs the fantasy went far beyond what had happened in reality.

She was wrecked. Bedevilled by a man who wanted nothing more to do with her. And the pain which scraped inside her was inexpressible.

She could pretend it was because of the echoes it had of the one other man with whom she had been intimate—the boy who had fathered Nell.

But she knew it was more than that. *Tak* was more than that. In her whole life she had never imagined meeting anyone who made her body dance and resonate and exalt the way he had succeeded in doing.

So if she could just get through the next few days without having to see him, or at least without having to be alone with him… It was the only antidote she could think of.

'I thought maybe you might like to have a girls' weekend with me,' Effie said, and laughed brightly.

'Why?' Her daughter frowned, unconvinced.

'Why not?'

Nell twisted her mouth from side to side as if weighing up the options. 'Where did you even *get* that stuff, anyway? I can't see Dr Lover-man having a ready supply of fairy cake cases and all that.'

'I went shopping this morning. I also bought popcorn we can throw into the microwave as we gorge on fun chick-flicks on that enormous cinema screen downstairs.'

'What is going *on* with you?' Nell cried. 'You don't even *like* baking.'

'I do,' Effie objected. 'I just like eating what's at the end of the process far more than the actual process. Now, can you just show me how to crack these eggs into the flour without getting shell in it?'

They were halfway through a mess when Tak walked in.

'How's the cake-baking?'

'Fine!' Effie declared a touch maniacally.

'Awful.' This from Nell.

He advanced into the kitchen with a grin and Effie was suddenly hit by an incredible urge to throw the electric mixer at him. If he was lucky she might actually turn it off first.

'What seems to be the trouble?'

'Nothing.' Effie tried again. 'No trouble.'

Nell eyed her impatiently. 'Mum has no idea how many eggs, or how much butter, flour and sugar to use. She also thinks any kind of flavouring is a luxury, rather than a prerequisite—including vanilla.'

'I see.'

'I'm fine,' Effie repeated, in a way that suggested that if she told herself enough times she might actually make it so.

'You're really *not*, Mum.'

'Effie, come on. Let me help.' he said. 'I've made a fair few cakes in my time—including birthday cakes.'

Nell, it seemed, had heard all she needed to.

'Fab. Here.' She had untied her apron and whipped it off in an instant. 'You take over. If I spend any more time in here with Mum one of us isn't going to make it out alive. And I'm afraid it might not actually be me.'

'Sorted.' Tak nodded, taking over as though there was nothing else he'd rather be doing on a Saturday evening. 'Okay, Effie, what do you want me to do?'

He really did look delectably divine, standing there.

'You can cream the eggs and sugar,' Effie managed at last, and she knew he'd heard the catch in her voice when a tiny frown creased his forehead.

She reminded herself that he couldn't read her thoughts. That only she knew the delicious secret she was holding inside at this moment.

'You've really made cakes?' Effie asked, after they'd been working together for a while.

'I have. Growing up, I found that baking cakes with Hetti and Sasha was a good way to get them to talk about any problems that they were having in school.'

'Is that how you knew the best way I should handle Nell?' The words tumbled out clumsily, as if she knew that if she didn't just *say* it she might lose her nerve. 'That night at the ball when we were talking about the shoplifting? Do you remember?'

'I remember.'

He should shut her down. Tell her it was none of his business. He would have done with anyone else. But Effie was different—even if he couldn't explain what made her so. A part of him wanted to tell her, and therein lay the dilemma. Because if he told her then he knew—just *knew*—that it would change things.

She would change things.

She would change *him*.

'Don't forget I have sisters,' he offered at last. 'Both of whom were teenagers in every sense of the word. I remember what it was like.'

'But it's more than that, isn't it?' she asked softly. 'You don't just remember things in the abstract, the way an older brother might recall. You *understand*. The way a parent who has really been through it might.'

Something dark and cutting and raw scraped within his chest, making even breathing become difficult. 'I have never been a parent. And I never intend to be one.'

'Which is what makes it all the more curious,' Effie whispered. 'The way you knew what to say that night. The way you couldn't stop yourself from checking that we were okay. The way you've taken charge of us now and brought us to your home.'

'It's simply looking out for a colleague.'

Any other person might have heeded the warning note in his voice. But not Effie. 'I don't think so.'

'Perhaps you want to think carefully about antagonising the person who has provided a roof over your head.'

It was a jagged threat couched in the silkiest of tones. He hated himself for playing the game.

But instead of acknowledging the danger and stepping back Effie stepped closer. Metaphorically and physically. Her voice slid under his skin.

'Or you'll do what? Throw me out on my ear? I don't think so; your sense of responsibility wouldn't allow it.'

How was it that he could barely breathe? His lungs were too constricted?

'You'd be foolish to mistake my professional attitude for my personal one. Where my job is concerned I take my responsibilities exceedingly seriously. But you must know that where my private life is concerned I dodge responsibility at every turn.'

'The trouble is I don't believe that.'

'I can't make you.'

He made himself lift his shoulders. In all his life no one aside from his siblings had ever made him want to reveal his true self before. No woman had ever got to him like this. What was it that made Effie so different? Like a law unto herself.

He could see something was whirling inside her, even if he couldn't be sure what that something was.

'Do you ever slow down?' he asked abruptly.

'Not if I can help it.'

It was possibly the most honest answer she could have given him.

'Why not?'

Effie bit her lip and Tak perched on a tall bar stool, prepared to wait it out.

'Why not, Effie?'

'Because if I slow down then I give myself a chance to stop, to think. And there's a part of me which doesn't want to do that.'

'Because then you'll end up thinking about where you are in your life and wondering if you'd made different choices where you might have been?'

'It drives me insane,' she frowned.

'It's allowed to.

'Not when it sometimes throws up more questions than answers. It ends up confusing everything.'

'It doesn't have to.'

'I suppose,' Effie conceded after a moment. 'But I wish it wasn't like that.'

'You're not alone.'

She stopped abruptly, waiting, wondering, and Tak suddenly found himself speaking—filling the silence—even though he'd had no intention of doing so.

'I had another brother, you know. Saaj. He was eight months old when he was diagnosed with a neurodegenerative disease. To this day we still don't know the cause, but my suspicion is that it was immunopathic.'

'I'm so sorry.'

Her tone was so sincere, so gentle, that he could feel the emotion balling in his throat. He waved her aside with his hand.

'Saaj spent most of the next fourteen months in hospital unconscious, or if he was conscious then he was usually in pain. And as a baby he couldn't articulate it. He was simply inconsolable, but unlike a normal baby there was nothing my mother could do to help him. She was there with him every day, but she couldn't talk to him, or comfort him, or even cuddle him, because as the illness progressed even that caused him too much pain.'

'Tak…'

She uttered his name softly. Neither a plea nor a statement, just a reassurance that she was there, and he realised that at some point she'd taken his hands, as though lending him support. He'd never thought he'd needed it. Until now.

'She was in hell—unable to comfort him and equally unable to take his pain away.'

He couldn't bring himself to tell her the truth about his mother. The way Saaj had been her excuse to abandon the rest of her children when they too had needed her. The way she'd already been doing before Saaj had been born. But with Saaj she'd had a clear-cut reason which no one—especially not his ten-year-old self—had been able to argue with.

And so he'd taken on the responsibility of caring for his siblings—from changing nappies to washing clothes and finding them something to eat every day. He'd hated his mother for not caring for them enough. And he'd hated his philandering father for caring for himself too much.

But what if Effie didn't believe him? Worse, what if she took his mother's side and decided he was being callous, lacking any empathy?

'What about your father?'

'He wasn't around.'

That was all Tak was willing to offer. What else was there to say? That his father had been so busy with his whores that he hadn't cared about anyone else?

'I was a kid. I took care of my siblings.' He wrapped it up neatly. 'That's why I don't want that life now. I don't want a family. I feel like I've already been there and had that. I love being a surgeon.'

'Baby Saaj is why you became a surgeon, though, isn't he?' she asked abruptly.

Her quiet but clear words cut through the air. Through him. Incredibly, Tak found he couldn't answer her. His tongue simply wouldn't work.

'And not just any surgeon.' Her eyes might as well be pinning him to the spot. 'But a neurosurgeon.'

She could read him in a way that no one else ever had. It should unnerve him more.

'If I wanted you to psychoanalyse me I'd get on

a couch and give you a clipboard,' he managed to bite out eventually. 'The point is that I don't need any distractions. I don't need a wife or a family at home, reminding me that I've let them down or abandoned them because I've got caught up with some case, some patient.'

It was intended as a conclusion, but she looked as though she was about to say more. He needed something to distract her. Words pressed urgently against his tongue, as if they were desperate to get out, whatever logic his brain might be using to restrain them.

'Come with me to the neurology conference in Paris,' he said. It certainly wasn't what he'd expected to say.

'No.' She shook her head at once.

'Why not?'

She eyed him apprehensively, as though trying to work it out. How he'd gone from shutting her out to inviting her to go away with him.

He was still trying to work it out himself.

'Nell's going on her ski trip at the same time,' he said. 'And you told me yourself that you've never been abroad but you've always wanted to. Here's your chance.'

She bit her lip and he had to fight the oddest impulse to draw it into his mouth and kiss her thoroughly, just as he had before. More.

'Where would I stay?'

It was as though she could read his every salacious thought where she was concerned.

'I'll get you a separate room.'

'Won't everything be booked up with the conference?'

Not if he flashed his credit card and offered them extortionate sums to solve the problem.

'I can ask…' He shrugged.

'But you won't think I…? You won't expect…?'

She flushed and he knew exactly what she was trying not to say.

'Effie, I can assure you there will be no expectations on my part. We got it out of our systems the other night. Now we can go back to how it was before.'

'You think so?'

'I do,' he asserted, wishing he felt half as sure as he sounded.

'Well, okay, then.'

She smiled. A gentle half-smile which blew him away.

'If you're sure?'

'Sure.' He nodded.

Only he wasn't sure. Not at all. Where Effie was concerned he couldn't seem to control himself.

But this time he had no choice.

CHAPTER TWELVE

EFFIE STRODE THROUGH the hotel lobby, through the doors and practically skipped down the steps and away from the stuffy, windowless, airless conference room.

She stopped abruptly and tipped her head up. The sun was glorious in a cloudless blue sky. Like every stunning glossy magazine photo she'd ever seen all rolled into one.

Only better.

Not just because she was actually here, rather than merely standing holding a holiday brochure and imagining she was, but also because of the man who had brought her here.

For the best part of a week she'd been nodding courteously to Tak when she'd seen him at the hospital, smiling politely at him when he'd passed by whatever room she and Nell had been in at his home, and chatting amicably to him whenever actually meeting him had been unavoidable.

She absolutely, definitely, categorically had *not* been imagining him kissing and licking her, turning her inside out and making her cry out with unabashed abandon as she climaxed over and over again.

Shaking her head—her hair was wild and free, as it so often seemed to be these days—Effie tried to eject the memories from her head. She was here, in Paris, without a single other person to think about. She could do whatever she wanted, whenever she wanted to.

So, where to go first? Effie wondered, picking one cobbled street at random. Would she find herself in a square full of artists, all gathered together to share their creativity, or perhaps the famous cabaret house of the Moulin Rouge, or perhaps she'd even stumble upon Montmartre Cemetery, the last resting place of literary greats like Zola or Dumas?

She wound through the streets, scarcely able to believe she was here—*abroad*. It felt so different from anything she might have anticipated and yet simultaneously exactly as thrilling, from the sights and sounds to the language itself.

Effie had no idea how long she'd wandered, taking in a museum here or a sculpture there, wandering in the footsteps of Picasso and Van Gogh, when suddenly she rounded on a tiny *crêperie*, squashed between bigger, sturdier, architecturally more attractive buildings, and the mouth-watering smells lured her inside.

By the time she exited, sugary crumbs from her glorious hot treat still coating her lips, she felt like a kid again, practically skipping up the steps she saw opposite her. Steps and steps and yet more steps.

And suddenly there she was, with the white

dome of the Sacré-Coeur, Montmartre's sacred basilica, right in front of her. Like a perfect dollop of whipped cream in the dazzling sunlight. People were spread out everywhere—on the steps, in the grassy areas, even on walls and benches—laughing and happy and making her feel like a part of something without even saying a word to her.

Which made it all the more curious that Tak should once again sneak into her thoughts. That she should wonder what it might be like to visit a place like this as a couple. *With him.*

It didn't matter how much she pushed that night into a box and tried to turn the key on it, reminders always found their way out. Into her head and her chest, until she ached for him all over again.

Stalking away, as if she could somehow outpace it, Effie's eyes alighted on a caricaturist impressively capturing the fun, carefree young girl who was willingly posing for him. Her friends were jostling to be next as they gasped and admired the image.

It was a symbol of all the things Effie had never, ever been able to be, let alone when she was their age. She'd spent her entire life just trying to stay safe and under the radar. Watching other people have fun but never being able to enjoy it for herself.

She even held herself back with Tak—with the exception of the other night—and suddenly Effie couldn't help but wonder what she thought she was achieving by it. Was she protecting herself, as her head would argue, or was she in fact depriving herself of even a few snatched moments of something good for herself?

These few days in Paris with Tak were *her* time. And if she didn't seize the moment then who knew when it would present itself again?

'You look breathtaking,' Tak murmured as she met him that evening in the hotel bar, as per her own instructions.

She inclined her head to one side and just about kept her smile of delight from taking over her entire face. 'Thank you.'

She should hope so. An afternoon at a spa, and swimming, and even an indulgent visit to the hotel's hair salon had taken every bit of spare money she'd had. But it had been worth it to pamper herself for once. To feel as though she was being spoiled.

Carefully she took Tak's proffered arm and walked with him into the dining room, where the maître d' accompanied them to their table with economical gestures and an expansive smile and the sommelier fluttered around them as they made their wine selections.

The meal passed by pleasantly enough. Tak asked about her day, and in between her tantalising starter and succulent main course she told him about Abbesses, the Bateau-Lavoir, the Sacré-

Coeur. She kept to herself the lingerie boutique she'd visited on her way back from Montmartre. And after the cheese course was done and her dessert had arrived she enjoyed surprising him by telling him that she had eventually plucked up the courage to sit for a caricature.

Tak looked impressed. 'You'll have to let me see it.'

'Only if you promise not to laugh,' she warned him.

'Isn't that the point of a caricature? To amuse?'

'Yes,' she conceded, savouring her *crème brûlée*. 'But pleasantly.'

'Then I assure you I shall not laugh.' He managed to look solemn. 'And what about tomorrow?'

'Tomorrow I'm taking the Métro, and I'm going to visit the Eiffel Tower and walk along the Seine.'

'You could always come and join our team for a day. You could provide a different perspective for one of our talks—the first-on-the-scene account.'

'No, thanks!' Effie laughed. 'I'm here to play, not to work.'

'You haven't really ever had time to play, have you?' asked Tak, without warning. 'Time to yourself.'

'Have *you*?' she threw back softly. 'I mean, *really*? You have your games suite, and you see your brothers and sisters, but isn't it all really still your way of taking care of your siblings? You didn't buy that house for yourself, did you? You bought it for your sisters and your brother to live in with you until they had their own families. And you always meet up with Rafi because you want to check on him—although I'm not sure why.'

Something shimmered in the air between them. All around them was the hum of chatter, the clinking of glass and the scrape of cutlery against china.

It felt like an eternity, but then at last Tak answered her. 'You really want to know?'

'I do.'

He took a long drink of wine, quite unlike his usual carefulness. Effie stayed still. Patient.

'I told you about Saaj, and how I had to hold things together for my other siblings whilst my mother was with him,' he said. 'But I didn't tell you that he was a deliberate mistake. That my mother had him late in life as a way of trying to win my father back.'

'I don't understand…'

'My parents had an arranged marriage. She was a good match for my father and she was determined to be a good wife. But my father was handsome, a doctor, and to some a meal ticket. He had women throwing themselves at him and he was weak and greedy and he wanted it all. A very proper wife back home, having his children and raising his family, and a naughty young mistress who would do all the dirty things with him he felt a wife should not do.'

Every word cut into her. Tak's mother might have suffered a different fate from herself, but ultimately it was still rejection, betrayal. She couldn't imagine what Tak's mother must have gone through.

A thought occurred to her. 'Did your mother know?'

'Oh, she knew. She made excuses for him. Told us all that he was a clever, powerful man and that it was his entitlement—even though it killed her so much she used to self-medicate.'

'Tak, that must have been awful for her. For all of you.'

She wasn't prepared for the fury he directed at her.

'Don't make excuses for her! Everyone makes excuses for her. Including me. For years. But we were *there*—Hetti and Sasha, Rafi and I. We *lived* it. And what she did to us is inexcusable. I've finally started to accept that fact.'

For a moment she felt as if he'd shouted the words, hurling them at her with all the rawness and the pain he'd bottled inside for far too long. But one look around the oblivious diners at the restaurant told her that he had barely hissed them loudly enough for her to hear.

It didn't lessen their impact one iota.

'Tak, she must have felt so isolated...so alone—'

He cut her off before she could say any more.

'You have empathy because you're kind and you're caring. That's who you are, Effie. But in this case you're wrong. She didn't have to make excuses for him, or stay with him. She didn't have to put us, her children, through years of suffering because of their twisted relationship. But she did—because she was selfish.'

'Tak—' She stopped abruptly as the waiter arrived to clear their plates and bring them coffee.

All she wanted to do was send him away, so that she could talk to the man sitting stiffly, wretchedly, opposite her. Not that anyone else could see it but her. And what did that say about their relationship—or lack of one?

'No, Effie,' he snarled as they were finally left alone again. 'You feel for her because you think you see a parallel, but the two of you are nothing like each other. You went through far, far worse than my mother and yet look what you did. You put your daughter first from the instant she was born. You put her needs ahead of yours. You struggled alone through university, with a baby, because you knew that was your responsibility.'

'It isn't that simple,' Effie offered slowly. 'Not everyone is the same.'

'She could have left him. She had family—quite a lot of family—who would have supported her leaving with her children rather than staying with him. They knew he was cruel, and that he deliberately rubbed his affairs in her face. He even told me, *his son*, that he was more compatible in bed with any one of his whores than he was with my mother. Despite the fact they'd had four children together.'

Effie hesitated. With Saaj, that was five children, which meant it had been going on long before Saaj had been born.

'*Now* you're getting it.' Tak laughed, but it was a hollow, grating sound. 'Yes, he was throwing those insults about, sleeping with his tarts, and my mother was still weak enough to let him into her bed. Still stupid enough to believe that if she fell pregnant one more time he would finally come to his senses and realise that he wanted to be a family man, after all.'

'She always hoped he would change,' Effie whispered sadly. 'But he was never going to.'

'Of *course* he was never going to,' Tak scorned. 'Which was why she spent fifteen years medicating herself into oblivion and leaving *me* to raise *her* children when I was still a child myself. I was ten when I first took over responsibility for them. When really I needed her just as much.'

'Is that why you're so adamant about never marrying? Never letting anyone close? Because you've already practically raised a family and now you want to reclaim the childhood you lost?'

Somehow that didn't fit the Tak she knew.

'I don't want a family because I don't want to do to anyone what my father did to my mother.'

He bit the words out, stunning her into silence. For a moment Effie couldn't move. And then she sucked a breath in. 'Why would you even think you would do that? That isn't you at all.'

'I'm more like my father than you know,' Tak countered darkly. 'My mother said so often enough when I was growing up.'

And all of a sudden it was desperately, painfully clear to Effie. In her despair and devastation and depression, his mother had taken all her fears out on her oldest son. Perhaps it had been her way of venting, or perhaps it had been her way of ensuring her son wouldn't turn on her, but Effie could imagine it in crystal-clear detail. A half-out-of-it mother screaming at her ten-year-old son that he was just like his father. She'd seen it often enough. Hell, she'd even lived it herself.

No doubt whenever Tak had voiced anything about doing something for himself—from playing a game of football with his friends, or going to a friend's house—anything which had meant he might not be there to care for his younger siblings, his mother would have thrown that accusation at him. Saying the one thing she knew would get the reaction he needed, likening him to the one person who disgusted him the most.

In spite of all that Tak had told her, and the empathy she had for his mother's situation, for that part of it Effie couldn't forgive her. A mother was supposed to look out for her children, love them, protect them. Tak's mother had made Tak responsible for his father's shortcomings, and she'd used his father against him every time he'd looked as if he was going to step out of line. She had damaged him emotionally. It had been cruel and it had been entirely avoidable.

And now all Effie could think was that she wanted to be the one to help Tak see the truth. To heal him. She didn't know if she could. She didn't know if anyone could. But she'd be damned if she didn't at least try.

'You aren't your father, Tak,' she offered softly.

'I know that,' he growled. 'But I'm his son. It's there somewhere. I have his genes.'

'You and I both know the nature versus nurture debate. You're a completely different person to your father. To both your parents, for that matter. Look at Hetti and the rest of your siblings.'

'Rafi is like him,' Tak ground out.

'Sorry?'

'Rafi. He lived through the same childhood I did. He knew exactly how that man destroyed everything. He hated him every bit as much as I did. And then, six months after he got married, I discovered he was having an affair. That he'd had a mistress on the side before he even got engaged.'

It took her a moment, but she finally thrust her shock aside. 'That still doesn't make *you* like him, Tak. It isn't what you stand for.'

'You can't know that for certain.'

'I can. Because that isn't who you are.'

But it was pointless. The conversation was over and Tak had shut her out. Again.

They sipped their coffee in silence, with Tak clearly marking time until he deemed it polite to leave. And then they were in the lift, the silence almost suffocating her as she stood next to him. He was only inches away and yet it might as well have been a whole continent. His fury and resentment were coming off him in waves.

He didn't so much walk her to her room door as stalk there, barely waiting for her key card reader to flash green before marching to his own door.

'Goodnight,' she ventured as she stood just inside her room.

But he was already gone.

For several protracted minutes Effie paced up and down in her sitting area. It was hell knowing he was only on the other side of that wall but that he was shutting her out. Torturing himself with accusations that should never have been hurled at him. Believing himself to be the kind of man who would do something which so disgusted him.

And what kind of willpower did it take to hold himself back from people—girlfriends—the way he must have done all his life?

Much the same as the willpower you've shown, a small voice whispered in the back of her head. *And was it really so difficult to stand back before Tak walked into your life?*

The thought lent her strength. What if *she* was to Tak what *he* had been to her? The one person to break through those barriers? She felt as though her day alone in Paris had unleashed something in her which hadn't been there for almost two decades. She felt wild, reckless and free. Maybe now it was time to put it to the test.

She didn't give herself time to think, lest she talked herself out of her. Talked herself back down to being the woman she always was—never seizing what she really wanted. And she wanted Tak.

Effie marched to the connecting door and slid the bolt, pretending she didn't see her hand shaking before she lifted her chin and strode through into Tak's room.

It was empty.

For a moment Effie hesitated. Did she turn back? Wait? Where *was* he, even?

And then she heard a door open around the corner and Tak walked in, with a damp sheen on his body, wet hair, and a small towel around his waist. He stopped, stared, and Effie didn't miss the tiny flare of his nostrils or the way his eyes widened a fraction.

It restored her waning courage and she propelled herself forward, towards him, stopping inches from his face. 'Pleasant shower?'

She couldn't resist lifting her hands, allowing them to skim over the glorious pectoral muscles of his well-honed chest. Her insides turned to mush just at this mere contact. Her only comfort was that she could feel coolness coming off his skin. A cold shower? Surely that had to be a good sign? As was the slightly hoarse edge to his voice when he spoke.

'What are you doing, Effie? I didn't bring you here for this.'

'No, I know. But still, I wanted to come and thank you for bringing me to Paris.'

He blinked, clearly surprised. She didn't blame him. She sounded bold, sensual—so unlike herself.

'You've already thanked me.'

'Well, I wanted to thank you properly.'

Before he could say anything else she tipped her head forward and pressed a kiss to the hollow at his throat, her hands tracing the rigid contours of his torso, her fingertips deliberately grazing his nipples.

And he let her. Not even moving as she dropped a trail of kisses from his neck downwards. His lack of reaction might have concerned her, but his breathing was too harsh, too shallow, and it betrayed him.

She inched closer, felt the unmistakable evidence of his growing arousal pressing instantly against her hip just as she heard the catch of breath in his throat. He hadn't been rejecting her at the door before—he'd been trying to respect her. But there was no doubt that he wanted her—*really* wanted her—as much as she wanted him.

It made her feel powerful, suddenly. In absolute control. Before he could stop her she hooked her fingers around the towel, unsecured it and then dropped to her knees in front of him. Finally a side of herself which she'd always wished she had was making itself known.

And it was all because of Tak Basu.

Her head was spinning with desire. With exultation. With the way Tak was completely at her mercy and apparently more than happy to be so. He was male—so utterly, gloriously, solidly male—and yet he was letting her do whatever she wanted to do to him.

It felt intoxicating to be entrusted with such power, such control. And, whatever happened next, she was determined that she would have this one perfect night with him.

CHAPTER THIRTEEN

HE SHOULD STOP HER.

Dimly the thought moved around Tak's head. But he couldn't. Not when she was kissing him, licking him, *torturing* him the way she was right now. An exquisite kind of torture which he thought might be the perfect death of him.

And then she took him in her hand, tilting her head up to him, her eyes clear and wanton, her lips curled up mischievously, and he felt a kick, low and hard, in his abdomen.

But that was nothing compared to the blow that hit him when she opened her mouth and took him deep inside her mouth. A blow which almost felled him.

He couldn't even breathe.

Effie. *His* Effie.

He couldn't say it. He had no right even thinking it. But she undermined his walls with every conversation and every revelation. And now with every wicked flick of her tongue. She was so incredibly perfect, and all he could do was thrust his hands into her hair in some kind of attempt to root himself to the ground, to keep himself from exploding there and then.

Slow and lazy at first, her mouth and her tongue were playing, teasing, toying with him.

Every flick of her tongue sent rivers of need cascading through his entire body, drowning out every other thought in his head. Carefully, she built up the pace. Taking her time as though she was enjoying every second of the lethal control she had over him.

And she *did* have control over him, Tak realised with a jolt, and not just because she had her mouth wrapped around him in this moment. She'd been gaining dominance over him every day since that first night at the hospital gala. Making him wish he really was a different man from the one he'd always feared he might be. He hadn't done a damn thing to stop it, and now he feared he never could.

She was under his skin, in his veins. Her touch, her scent, her voice. And he never wanted to let her go.

Her teeth grazed gently over his tip and with a start Tak realised he was embarrassingly close to losing himself.

'Stop,' he bit out. 'Not this way.'

It took everything he had to brace his fingers against her and pull back, hoisting her up into his arms as he did. His fingers were reaching for her zipper and releasing her from her dress until she was standing there in just her underwear. Not that it helped.

The black lace bra and brief set with its tiny

red bows would have been enough—feminine yet seductive, transparent enough for him to see everything. But then his eyes dropped to the matching suspender belt, the sheer stockings which only seemed to emphasise those impossibly long, sexy legs, and the heels which enhanced already shapely calves.

It was a devastating collection. Heady in the extreme. And Tak couldn't contain himself any longer.

In one move he scooped her into his arms, carrying her to the bed and lowering her as softly as his throbbing, aching body would allow before nestling between her legs and pressing his mouth to her where she needed him the most.

She was feverishly hot, magnificently wet, honey-sweet. She gasped instantly, bucking her hips, making him feel more turned on than he thought he'd ever been in his life. More desperate for her than he'd known possible.

'Tak…'

'Call it payback,' he growled, sliding his hands beneath her rounded peachy bottom and lifting her to him again. Wrapping those incredible legs around his shoulders. 'And I intend to exact every last bit. With interest.'

Then he hooked the fabric of her briefs to one side and simply licked into her. Over and over as she moved against his mouth and on his tongue.

The guttural sounds ripped from her throat were becoming more urgent and more needy by the second. And he didn't think he would ever be able to get enough of her. Of this. He traced whorls around her core with his tongue and his fingers, slipping them inside her, revelling in her gasps and the way she opened herself up to him as if she couldn't help herself. All the while maintaining a steady flick over the tiny bud at her core and stoking the fire which burned so brightly inside her.

And then he felt her changing, beginning to pull away. He heard a weak protestation on her lips, something about wanting to do this together, and Tak couldn't help himself. He held her in place and sucked deep and hard at her core, refusing to let her go.

Instantly her body trembled, and stiffened, and finally shattered all around him. She was exploding as though he'd driven her beyond all control, crying out his name as though she knew it too.

'I didn't want it this way,' she whispered regretfully when she finally came back to herself.

'Then you gave a rather good performance that you were enjoying it,' Tak murmured, standing above her, his desire still painfully obvious.

Effie struggled to lift herself on to her elbows. 'I don't mean I didn't enjoy it.' She blushed prettily. 'I think it's obvious that I did. More than enjoy it. I just meant I wanted both of us to…'

'We don't have protection,' he ground out, wishing his body wasn't urging him to ignore such a substantial obstacle. 'I didn't bring anything. I told you—I didn't bring you to Paris for this.'

And he had no intention of sleeping with anyone else whilst he felt this way about Effie. What did that say about their non-relationship?

'But *I* came prepared.' She offered a wry smile, fishing something out of her bra.

It took him a moment to recognise it for what it was. Then something slammed into his chest. Hard.

'Then it's a good job I'm not finished.'

Her eyes flew to his and she twisted her mouth nervously. For the first time it occurred to Tak that but for that one time in her youth—a one-off fumble which had resulted in Nell—Effie had no idea what she was doing.

For some reason that knowledge ignited some primal sense inside himself. She was rare, unique, otherwise untouched. She'd kept herself that way out of her own choice. She truly was *his*.

With a groan, he took the small packet from her fingers, lowering himself on the bed and moving over her body, his arms either side of her bearing his weight. Every inch of him was alive to every touch. Revelling in the way her hands roamed his body constantly, as though she couldn't get enough either.

She skimmed her hands over his chest, then his shoulders, and down over his back, tracing his braced shoulder muscles and the way his body tapered to his waist.

For his part, he feasted on her mouth, taking his time, giving her the chance to come down from her orgasm and beginning the process of building her up to another. He rained kisses on her face, on the bridge of her nose, over her eyebrows and to her temples. He pressed his lips to the sensitive spots below her ear and at her throat until her nails dug into his shoulders and she whispered for more.

Tak was only too happy to oblige.

He bent his head, pulling down one bra cup to expose her breast, which he kissed and licked and finally sucked, and then turned his attentions to the other. Back and forth, he ignored the throb of his desire, the way he ached to plunge himself so deep inside her that neither of them would know where he ended and she began.

The rawness, the need with which he wanted Effie, was like nothing he'd ever experienced before. Not least when she shifted and he nudged against her wetness. He feared he might be lost there and then.

It took him moments to open the wrapper and deftly slide on the condom, but it felt like an age, and then he settled back between her legs and eased himself close to her, his hand reaching down to stroke her silken folds and ensure she was ready.

He wasn't prepared for her to wrap herself around him and draw him quickly inside, her muscles stretching around him as though she'd been made exclusively for him, clenching over him, her heat making him sear.

'Easy, Effie...' He barely managed to get the warning out.

'I can't.' She lifted her hips, as though a slave to the rhythm they were setting on their own, completely independent of her. 'I want this. I've wanted this for so long.'

As her hands moved down his back to clutch his backside, as if she must drive him even deeper inside her, Tak couldn't stand it any longer. He slammed into her hard, again and again, and her cries urged him on as she rode out every wave with him. He moved his hand between them, stroking her, never letting up, and when he felt a shiver ripple through her body he pressed down hard and felt her orgasm take over.

For a while, he made himself hold on. Throwing her off the edge all by herself and watching her plummet, then soar. Waiting as she came back down to him. But before she could land he gave himself up to the moment, climaxing into her with a primitive sound which didn't even sound like himself.

This time when she took flight he soared with her.

And he never wanted to come back to the ground.

'It really must be something to be the King of Awake Craniotomies,' Effie pondered at some point in the early hours, after he'd reached for her several times more, sating her, exhausting her, and then doing it all over again.

'Hmm…?'

'All those people at the conference today. They all came to hear you speak.'

'There were lots of speakers there.'

'But it was you who packed the room. It was your speech which had the applause practically raising the roof off this hotel.'

'I've always thought, in many ways, that I'm lucky,' he replied eventually. 'People come to me when there's already a fair suspicion that there's a brain or spinal issue. But you, out there in the field, you never know what you're going to get. You have to be ready for anything, thinking of everything, catering to all possibilities.'

'It's…frightening sometimes,' she admitted. 'But it's also rewarding. Especially when a patient and his family make a trip to the air ambulance base months later to thank you for what you did. But you must get that, too.'

'Yes. Still, I'd love to see it from your perspective.'

'So come along.'

Effie shrugged, as if they were in a real relationship. As if considering the future wasn't strange. As if meeting up in a month or so, when she was back in her flat and any non-relationship she'd ever had with Tak wouldn't be awkward.

'We do ride-alongs for press and medical professionals sometimes. You could join us for a day. Because of your expertise you could probably even take the place of one of my paramedics for the shift.'

And he nodded, and kissed her thigh, and told her he would arrange it as soon as they got back. Then he reached for her again, already hard, already wanting her. Just as he would for the rest of the weekend.

And Effie—as foolish as she knew it was, she couldn't stop—wished it never had to be over.

CHAPTER FOURTEEN

'GEORGE IS SEVENTEEN years old. Half an hour ago he was with a group of friends climbing on Thor's Rock when he missed his footing and fell approximately eight feet onto a raised ledge.'

The paramedic from the land ambulance met Effie, Tak and the rest of the air ambulance crew at the base of the rock.

'He landed on his backside around thirteen feet up from here, on a raised ledge, and there's suspected spinal compression. He was apparently unconscious for approximately fifteen seconds.'

Effie nodded as she calculated the easiest way up the sandstone structure.

'He has severe pain in his lower back, and a pins and needles sensation in his legs. We've administered ten milligrams of morphine. Marco, the other paramedic, is up there holding the lad's head and spine straight so that he doesn't move. We were in the area—we were one of a couple of crews heading out to another incident—and they diverted us here instead.'

She nodded again, then turned to James, her own paramedic, and to Tak, who had chosen today to accompany them, just as they'd talked about in Paris.

It was impossible to pretend to herself that it

didn't feel significant. It was an unspoken ac-
knowledgement that their relationship wasn't just
about sex—which they'd enjoyed night after night
since their trip together—but about connecting
in the real world as well.

Slowly, bit by bit, she was beginning to shake
the fear that it could never last. That this shred
of happiness was bound to be ripped from her
the way that everything else bar Nell had been.

'It should be simple enough for us to get to the
patient.' She spoke quietly. 'There are quite a few
people already milling around up there, including George's friends, so clearly there's plenty of
room on the ledge. However, getting him down—
likely on a spinal board—will be a very different matter.'

'We have Mountain Rescue on hand to help,'
James pointed out. 'I can start sorting that out.'

'Good. Okay—Tak, you come with me. We'll
get up there and see what's going on,' She located
her first hand- and foot-holds and began making
her way up, reaching the ledge more quickly than
she'd anticipated, with Tak right alongside her.

'Hi, George—I'm Effie, the air ambulance doctor. How are you feeling?'

Within minutes Effie had completed her first
round of checks. The lad was clearly in a bad way,
and getting him down was going to be tricky for
both the crews and George himself.

'He can't straighten his legs, so we can't get

him onto the board and therefore we can't get him down.'

'Quite a severe mechanism of injury,' Tak murmured. 'I suspect a broken pelvis and spinal damage.'

'Yep—and time is ticking by. I'm going to administer ketamine, just so that we can get him onto a board. We're really going to have to be careful getting him down. The last thing I want is for anyone to slip on the rocks trying to lower him. It could end up causing him even more damage.'

'Understood. Do you want to put him in a pelvic brace?'

'Yes.' Effie bobbed her head.

Tak was every bit as proactive as she would have expected. And the way they worked together was so easy, so harmonious. It was a constant battle not to keep reading too much into it. Or into the fact that, even though they'd returned from Paris a week ago, her relationship with Tak didn't seem to have slowed for even a heartbeat. Even the level of discretion needed to keep Nell from realising the truth only seemed to have added a delicious air of adventure to it.

'You'll need to cut his joggers off,' she instructed, shaking the thoughts from her head.

But when Tak showed the scissors already in his hand and grinned, clearly on the same page, her stomach still flip-flopped deliciously.

'Good. Tak, I'm going to need you to help organise the Mountain Rescue teams onto staggered ledges, as equal in strength and height as you can, so that moving him out of here is as smooth as possible.'

'Sure.'

'Okay.' She nodded, plastering a smile on her lips and heading back to her patient. 'Right, George, what do think? Fancy a ride in a helicopter today?'

Effie tried not to skip downstairs the following morning, clad only in one of Tak's pristine bespoke shirts.

It was ridiculous that she felt so happy. Ridiculous, and amazing. A few days ago she could never have imagined herself sneaking down to a man's kitchen in order to prepare the two of them breakfast—or in her case something which might resemble breakfast. Least of all imagine sneaking into a man's kitchen after having made a superhuman effort to resist joining him whilst he stood in his huge walk-in shower. Never mind 'two-person'—an entire coachload could fit in it.

She was still smiling to herself as she practically danced along the hallway and through the wide archway—only to come to a sharp halt.

If she could have backed up, cartoon-like, then she would have. For there could be no doubt that the older woman who was sitting elegantly at the counter, sipping coffee from a bone china cup and saucer, was anyone other than Tak's mother.

Effie tugged ineffectively at the hem of Tak's shirt—the wearing of which now seemed like the stupidest idea she'd ever had. The woman's head turned slowly to meet her, her lips pulling instantly into a tight, disapproving line.

'Ms Robinson, I take it?'

A statement, not a question. And a less than enamoured one at that. It was worse than any cold reception she'd ever encountered as a kid, and something seemed to snap inside Effie.

She made herself drop the hem, stand a fraction taller and meet her critic's gaze head-on. 'It's Miss, actually.' Polite but firm. Not a trace of that shake which rocked her from the inside.

'I beg your pardon?'

Clearly Tak's mother wasn't accustomed to being challenged.

'Miss—not Ms.' Effie even forced herself to smile. 'For the sake of clarity.'

The woman's eyes narrowed. Then, if we are being so...*clear*, I should point out that my son's shirt barely covers the fact that you aren't wearing any underwear.'

Effie felt physically ill. But she cranked her smile up a notch. The censure and disapproval meant nothing to her, she reminded herself over her thumping heartbeat. She didn't need validation from other people—she wasn't that young kid any more.

'I don't believe Tak knew you were intending to visit, or I'm sure he would have made sure he was here to welcome you.'

'He didn't. Hemavati gave me a key. I imagine she was concerned. I let myself in.'

Effie chose to ignore that. 'Then will you excuse me whilst I go and find him?'

It wasn't really a question, but the woman darted her hand out to snatch Effie's arm, her grip decidedly painful.

'You mean *warn* him,' she replied evenly. 'No, I don't think so. My daughter told me you are staying because your flat is uninhabitable?'

'The boiler broke down and asbestos was found. The ceilings needed to be repaired and the central heating needed to be re-plumbed throughout.' It was all Effie could do not to cringe as the words came out. How easily it could sound like an excuse.

'I see. And Talank offered you his home?'

'He did.' Effie wrinkled her nose, imagining how that must sound.

'And, tell me, how long do you expect it to take? This repair?'

Effie felt too hot, then too cold.

'Actually, it was all done last Friday.'

'So…let me see…four days ago?'

Effie loathed the way the older woman made

such a dramatic show of counting back the days. She smiled cheerfully and made herself sound as breezy as she could.

'Must be, yes. Anyway, I should leave you to enjoy your morning drink in peace.'

Tak's mother smiled, though it was too sharp, too edgy to be sincere. And still it locked Effie in place.

'I wouldn't dream of it. Sit down—tell me about yourself and how you met my son. I understand that you're a doctor, too?'

She could still go. Ignore the woman's instructions, turn around and leave. Tak's mother was intimidating enough, without the fact that Effie was hardly even dressed. But if she went it would feel like a retreat, or that she had something to be ashamed of. And Effie couldn't explain it, but she didn't want to feel ashamed of anything that had happened between her and Tak.

And so she stayed, quietly moving around the kitchen to make herself a coffee and then discreetly pulling the shirt as low as possible and sliding into the seat across the table from Mrs Basu.

Only then did she finally speak.

'I'm a trauma doctor with the air ambulance,' Effie confirmed neutrally. 'I take patients to several hospitals in the area, including the Royal Infirmary.'

'Quite an impressive career. You don't look much older than Hemavati.'

Effie recognised the test. She offered a light laugh, as if she hadn't noticed. 'Hetti's barely twenty-six. It's many years since I was that young.'

'I see.' The other woman sipped her coffee carefully. 'So, then, are you all about your career, like Talank, or do you imagine yourself having a family?'

'You don't need to answer that, Effie.'

Effie jumped at the sound of Tak's voice over her head.

'That's an incredibly personal question, Mama.'

'Talank.'

The older woman's eyes narrowed as she tilted her cheek up for her son to kiss. Tak obliged, albeit stiffly, formally. It was a duty and a mark of respect, but not a sign of love. More than she would manage with her own mother, though.

For a moment Effie's stomach knotted into a tight ball. What must it be like to have a mother look at you differently? Feel differently about her child? Tak hadn't had it and neither had she. Did Nell know how much *she* was loved? Effie panicked. Had she succeeded in ensuring her daughter felt it every day of her young life?

Before she could stop herself, Effie opened her mouth. 'Actually, I already have a family, Mrs

Basu. I have a daughter. Eleanor. Although I usually call her Nell.'

'You have a baby?' The woman's gaze slammed into her like a hard, stinging slap.

It was all Effie could do not to raise her hand to her cheek, to check that the older woman hadn't, in fact, made contact. She took a moment to breathe, but to her surprise, Tak stepped in seamlessly.

'Nell is thirteen. She's a warm, friendly young girl, and a credit to Effie.'

'Is she here?'

'Effie and Nell were here whilst the repairs to their home were being dealt with.' He inclined his head, his tone firm, smooth. 'They moved back last week. Not that it's any of your concern.'

Tak's mother's eyes narrowed, as if in triumph. 'So you've left a thirteen-year-old girl alone in an apartment whilst you and her mother *frolic* here?'

It was bait, and even though everything in her screamed at her not to rise to it Effie felt her face heat with anger. 'Nell's at a friend's house,' she snapped. 'It's her friend's birthday and she's having a sleepover. And I am not *frolicking.*'

'Do you have a reason for coming here, Mama?' Tak demanded, his tone clipped.

Effie felt him cover her hand with his soothing touch.

'Or are you simply at a loose end because Father has dragged you over to the UK for some conference or other?'

It might have been phrased as a question but Effie knew an accusation when she heard one. And Tak's voice invited no further challenge.

'Are you comfortable?'

He turned to Effie with a wry smile. It was a shared moment which probably meant nothing to him yet it made something in her chest mushroom with happiness.

'Or would you prefer to leave?'

'I have a busy day.' Effie moved carefully out of her seat, grateful to Tak for providing her with the opportunity to leave. 'I might go and get ready now.'

'You're going to leave...*her* to roam around your home unsupervised?'

The implication was clear—*watch the family silver*—and Effie felt a tight band constrict around her chest. It was an accusation she'd heard enough times before, as she went into different foster homes. She hadn't felt that dirt-poor and pathetic in years. It was testament to just how manipulative this woman was that she'd located Effie's vulnerability within barely a five-minute conversation.

'Effie,' Tak corrected. 'Not *her*. And, yes, she knows the layout of the house well enough not to need a guide—but it's very thoughtful of you to be concerned in case Effie becomes lost.'

Effie flinched on his mother's behalf. She recognised that tone, and it wasn't as neutral as it seemed. The undercurrent and the subtle put-down made her skin bump. His mother had pursed her lips, as though she knew it, too.

For a moment silence descended on the room as the woman clearly burned with curiosity and Tak merely busied himself with breakfast. Completely at ease, the King of the Castle. Just as he was king everywhere he went.

She should go. Escape the tension. Instead Effie hovered in the doorway, unable to bear the thought of herself being the cause of disharmony between mother and son. And still his mother stared at the deliberately laid-back Tak, as if her eyes boring into him could somehow reveal all the answers which she was clearly so desperate to know.

An age dragged past, though it was probably less than a minute, and finally Effie excused herself.

She had no idea whether the words which followed her down the corridor came because his mother thought she was out of earshot, or because the older woman intended her words to be overheard.

'You're using her, Talank. *I* can see it, but does *she* know it?'

There was the briefest of pauses and Effie

couldn't help it. She slowed her pace, wishing fervently that she could see Tak's face.

'I will concede that when Effie and I first got together it was something of a mutual arrangement. A buffer, shall we say?'

As much as she knew it was the truth, Effie wasn't prepared for the shard of regret which stabbed through her.

'A buffer?' his mother replied coldly.

'Why not? Clearly you already know this, Mama. You wouldn't be here if Hetti hadn't already spoken to you. She *did* explain it all, didn't she?'

'You sister mentioned some mutual agreement, I suppose. Something about you and that woman both being single…'

'You are my mother, and as such I try to respect you. But if you wish me to continue this conversation,' Tak interjected, his voice quietly dangerous, 'then you will refer to Effie by her name. Am I making myself clear?'

'You don't respect me, Talank. You never have. Have you?'

He ignored the question. 'Am I making myself clear?'

'Effie, then,' his mother bit out coldly.

Clearly she didn't like it. It was surely testament to Tak's authority that she nevertheless obeyed.

'There, now, was that so difficult?'

Still immobile in the corridor, Effie realised she didn't want to linger there, eavesdropping. She didn't want to hear any more. She was genuinely afraid of what might be said. Tak's voice was barely recognisable. It held a tone she'd never heard before. A tone she never wanted to hear directed at *her*.

She tried to force her legs to move, but they felt rooted to the spot. As though they might fold if she attempted to force them.

'According to Hemavati, you and… *Effie*—' Effie could practically hear the gritted teeth '—were only together for show. To redirect attention for an evening.'

'Originally, yes.'

'Your sister also believes that you only invited *Effie* here—and now I discover her daughter as well—because she had nowhere else to go.'

'Is this conversation going somewhere relevant? I was under the impression that I could do whatever I chose, given that it is my *own* home. Or would you rather I'd seen them out on the streets?'

'I would rather hear that you had told *Effie* that it wasn't an action made out of the goodness of your heart so much as you making her and her daughter pawns in your quarrel against me. And against your father.'

'You talk about him as though you're a *team*,' Tak spat out instantly.

Something in his tone had Effie spinning around, as though she could hurry back down the corridor. As though she could somehow soothe his pain.

'He's never been a team player. Not for you. Not for anyone.'

'He loves me in his own way,' his mother hissed furiously. 'If it hadn't been for my becoming a mother—if it hadn't been for *you*—then he would have wanted me for a lot longer.'

'He *never* loved you—can you really not see that?' Tak roared. 'He is selfish and cruel and he only loves himself. He has only ever loved himself.'

'And you are just like him,'

The accusation hung in the air like a knife thrown at a spinning board just as time was frozen. Effie couldn't move. If she did then she might race back down to that kitchen, take that virtual knife and stab that woman right in the heart with it. The way *she* had been stabbing at Tak all these years, trying to beat him into submission with her cruelty, her callousness.

How he had become such a decent, compassionate man in the face of it all was a miracle.

'If you think that, Mama,' Tak managed icily, 'then why push me for an arranged marriage? If I'm so like him, how could you want to put some innocent bride through everything you went through?'

'Because, contrary to what *I* know of you, people think you're a catch, Talank. And your father will benefit from a lot of contacts if we make the right match. You owe us that much. You can keep this tramp of yours on the side, if you really need to.'

Effie could feel Tak's fury even from where she stood. His mother's words might have cut into her, but every time Tak defended her it felt like the most soothing of balms.

'Effie is not a tramp. And if I were to marry anyone I would marry *her*. I would have no mistress. She would be enough.'

'But you *aren't* going to marry her, are you, Talank?' his mother continued victoriously. 'And for all this noble talk of yours, you and I both know the truth, don't we? You didn't just choose Effie as this *mutual buffer* you claim. You chose her deliberately.'

There was no reason for Effie's blood to chill and slow in her veins, she told herself anxiously. No reason at all.

'Careful…' Tak warned.

But his mother had clearly smelled blood and now she was going in for the kill. Whether it was Tak or Effie, she didn't care. In any case, one equated to the other.

'You *chose* to align yourself with a woman who would sully your reputation by association.'

'That's enough.' Tak's voice was icy.

'She is unmarried with a child. Damaged goods. Even *you* couldn't carry that kind of toxic baggage and still be useful to your father and me.'

The truth slammed into Effie like a knee to the chest. Powerful enough to cause internal bleeding and even cardiac arrest. It catapulted her back to a time when she hadn't been good enough. When people had done everything they could to disassociate themselves from her and she had been wholly ashamed of who she was and where she'd come from.

But this time she had no one to blame but herself. From the start Tak had warned her that he would hurt her and she hadn't believed him.

More fool her.

'I warned you—that's enough!' he bellowed.

It was enough for Effie. The silence stretched out, straining, twisting, pulling taut. And with it came a tugging on her heart, until she felt as though it might tear in two.

She couldn't bear it any longer.

With her hand over her mouth to stifle any sound, she finally found her strength and raced up the corridor to her room. All she had to do was find her clothes and she would be out of there within minutes.

And she would never come back.

CHAPTER FIFTEEN

TAK EYED HIS MOTHER, feeling an odd, unexpected kind of fury building inside him. He ignored her question and the fact that he didn't—couldn't—answer her. He was only glad that Effie had left long enough ago that she wouldn't have heard that. It would have hurt her more than he could have borne.

'You will not repeat that to Effie. Ever,' he said with deliberate calm. 'Do you hear me? I don't know what you think you're doing here, but the time for me to pretend that you are any kind of mother is long gone. I made excuses for you because of Saaj, but you were never a mother in the truest sense of the word. Not to me, and not to the others. The only reason you mourned Saaj was because you had some twisted idea in your head that he was the key to winning my father back.'

Instead of paling and slumping in her seat, as he might have feared, his mother narrowed her eyes, drawing her face into an ugly, cruel expression. 'Is this *her* influence? Damaged, toxic, and now she causes you to speak to your *mama* that way?'

In one terrible instant the scales fell from Tak's eyes. He would never be able to reason with this person and he would never be able to save her.

She'd thrown her lot in with his father a long time ago and the man was like a wild, savage sea, with no respect for life or safety. Uma would drown because his father fed off her struggles. He sucked her under time and again, and she refused to right herself or grab hold of anything that could rescue her.

There was nothing Tak could do. Nothing anybody could do. She was anchored to him and she loved it.

But he wasn't going to let some sense of filial duty or honour tie him up any longer. He couldn't throw his mother out—that would be a step too far. But Effie had told him that he wasn't like his father and he was choosing to believe *her*. He was choosing *her*.

Turning his back on his ranting mother, he called Havers. 'Tell Effie we're leaving. We'll return as soon as my mother has left this house. And as soon as she is gone change the locks.'

'Effie has gone, Mr Basu.'

In all the time Tak had known the old man, he'd never seen him upset.

Time seemed to slow. 'What is it, Havers?'

'She looked rather *distressed*, sir.'

The room closed around Tak. Everything felt too tight, too constricting. Even his skin seemed to compress on his bones.

She had overheard. There could be no other explanation.

He turned to face his mother. The gleam of delight in her eyes was unmistakable.

'And so the mighty fall,' she proclaimed. 'All this disgust and disdain you show for your father, and all along I've warned you that you're just like him. That you will hurt any woman who doesn't know what she's getting herself into with you. All those names you've called him and all that hatred you have for him. How does it feel, Talank, to know that you *are* him?'

Tak didn't answer. He couldn't. It was as if a storm was closing in on him. It had come out of nowhere, so fast that he hadn't even known it existed before. But he was getting caught up in it now, and he didn't know which direction to even begin to turn.

How had he let himself believe he could be a better person? A man worthy of a woman like Effie? He should have gone with his gut—pushed her away the minute he knew something was happening between them.

But he'd known even from that first moment in Resus that there was something unique, something incredible about Effie. It had lured him in and it had seduced him. And he, in turn, had seduced her. Into his life and then into his bed. He'd taken advantage of her, and what was more he'd justified it by telling himself the attraction was mutual.

'You could go after her, Mr Basu,' Havers said suddenly. 'She would probably appreciate that.'

For a perfect instant Tak nearly obeyed. Then reality set in. He couldn't go to her now. That would only be rubbing salt into an already very raw wound. Calculating and insensitive. The best thing he could do now would be to stay away from Effie. To let her get back to her life and some semblance of normality.

Swinging around, Tak dismissed Havers and faced his mother. It took everything he had not to react to that cruel triumph radiating from her eyes.

'You may have won this round,' he told her, as evenly and as calmly as he could manage. 'But you won't win any more. Get out of my home and out of my life. I'm not my father and I never will be, and you'll need to find a new punch-bag. And if you go anywhere near Hetti or Sasha or Rafi I will make sure you regret it for the rest of your life.'

He didn't even wait for her to answer. He simply walked away. Out of the room. Out of the house. Into his car.

He didn't care if he drove all night or all week. As long as he stayed away from Effie—didn't hurt her any more than he already had—that was all that mattered.

* * *

'This is Maggie, thirty-four...' Effie briefed the team, relief pounding along her veins as she noted that Tak wasn't the neurological surgeon assigned to the case. 'At around six forty-five she was on a ladder, painting the first-floor window frames on her house, when she fell approximately four metres to the ground and landed on her back on a concrete path.'

In truth, she had no idea whether or not Tak was even in the hospital today. And she'd spent her entire shift—the entire past thirty-six hours, in fact—telling herself that she would never think about him again.

But it was like outlining a specific image and then telling someone not to instantly picture it in their head. Impossible.

'When we arrived GCS was thirteen, transmitted upper airway sounds equal air entry bilaterally, blood pressure was low and she was complaining of lower lumbar pain and looked very pale. Suspected internal bleeding. From top to bottom, she has a deep three-inch laceration to the head, lower back and pelvic pain, suspected spinal fractures. We administered one-fifty milligrams of ketamine for the pain.'

It might almost have been possible to lose herself in her cases, with shout after shout ever since she'd arrived at the air ambulance base at six o'clock that morning—if it hadn't been for the leaden ball filling her chest every single second.

She was grateful when the rest of the hand-over passed off without a hitch and she could get out of there. As soon as she got back to the base she would be done for the day. Maybe another night's sleep would finally begin to shake Tak from out of her head.

She snorted to herself. Well, she could live in hope.

'Effie.'

He caught her as she was exiting the building.

She wouldn't have stopped, but her legs refused to work and she didn't want to risk humiliating herself any further by forcing them to move only to collapse right there on the ground. Worse, have him pick her up in his arms.

She heard him jog up behind her and then move around to face her.

'I have to get back to base,' she managed. 'They're waiting for me on the heli.' But there was no concealing the quiver in her voice and she knew he heard it, too.

'No, they aren't. They've left. Your pilot was close to his maximum flying hours and he had to get back to base. You were still in the middle of the hand-over in Resus, and technically your shift finished an hour ago, anyway.'

'Oh.' She swallowed. 'Well, then, I need to get

back to my paramedics so we can head back together.'

'They've left too. I said I'd give you a lift back to your base and your car.'

Of course he had. A sliver of irrational anger cut through her. *Taking charge as if he had every right to do so.*

And then he opened his mouth and with two simple words took the heat out of everything.

'I'm sorry.'

She let the apology linger between them for a moment.

'What for?' she asked eventually, her voice soft. 'The fact that I'm damaged goods or the fact that you didn't tell me that was why you were using me?'

'She's gone, Effie,' he said quietly.

If she hadn't known better she'd have thought he was ashamed. But that was impossible, because Tak was *never* ashamed.

'She's out of our lives.'

The anger rushed back, flooding her. 'There is no *our lives*,' Effie exploded before she could check herself. 'You *used* me.'

'We used each other at the beginning,' he reminded her. 'That was the deal.'

It hurt. Too much.

'No, the deal was that we would be each other's buffer. The deal was never that because I was so damaged and toxic you would become tainted by association. I suffered enough of that growing up, because of my mother and where I was from. I will *not* accept it as a proud, hard-working single mother of a beautiful daughter.'

She wasn't prepared for him to reach out and snag her chin, forcing her to tip her head up, making her meet his eye.

'Nor *should* you accept it. Ever. But those were *her* words—they were never mine.'

'They might as well have been,' Effie argued, wrenching her head away, feeling the hurt blistering inside her like a chemical burn she couldn't get to. 'You gave her the weapon and you gave her the ammunition. You even marked me out as the target and you never even warned me. All she had to do was point and shoot.'

'I didn't even know you had a daughter when I asked you to that gala. Neither did Hetti. How could I have possibly chosen you on the basis she accused me of doing?'

He sounded rational, yet urgent all at once, and Effie realised there was some comfort to be taken from that. She felt her shoulders slump slightly, and there wasn't a thing she could do about it.

'You might not have intended it. At least not initially,' she conceded. 'But once you knew about Nell—once I told you that night at the gala—you must have known people would find out. You must have known this would be your family's reaction.'

He didn't deny it, although he looked as though he would give anything to, and there was some small comfort to be taken from that, too.

But then a horrid thought stole into her mind. 'Is that why you kissed me? After you'd assured me that everything would be platonic between us?'

'No!' he refuted instantly, a little too loudly for comfort. 'No. That isn't what happened. I kissed you because I wanted to. More than that, I couldn't stop myself. But I didn't intend to. I didn't plan it.'

'And that's where the problem lies, isn't it?' Effie smiled, but it was a weak, bitter smile. 'Because I don't believe you. I *can't* believe you. You could have told me at any time that Nell's existence had changed me from being your "buffer" to being your dirty little mistress, but you never did.'

He blanched at her words. Of course he did. Because she'd chosen them deliberately to really hit her point home. To hurt him. Anywhere near the amount he'd hurt her.

'*You're* the one who said I wasn't like him,' Tak said darkly. Thickly.

She wanted to stop but she found she couldn't. She had to ram the knife in a little bit deeper. 'That was when I thought I knew you. Now I know better.'

For the longest time he stood and stared at her.

And she wished she had even an inkling of what he was thinking.

'You were right,' he said hoarsely. 'I am nothing like him. I never was. It was just something my mother said to keep a desperate ten-year-old in line. But you're also right that I should have been more honest with you. I just never thought I would meet a woman who got under my skin as you do. And by the time I realised that you had it was too late to explain it all.'

'It would never have been too late,' Effie choked out. 'If it had come from *you*. Not some stranger. Not someone who wanted to cut me down. I've had enough of that throughout my life. If you had really cared for me you would have protected me from it happening again.'

'I tried to warn you that I'm not a good man.'

She felt buffeted and fragile. Pushed and pulled between hating him and…and something else which she didn't care to acknowledge.

'That's bull. You *are* a good man, Tak.'

It felt as though the words were being torn from her mouth. She felt compelled to tell him the truth, yet simultaneously she didn't want to leave herself any more vulnerable and exposed than she already was.

'I should never have said what I did. It was a low blow, and whatever has happened you don't deserve that. You're an incredible doctor, you care about your patients, and you go above and be-

yond. Every time. You're an amazing brother—
Hetti says so all the time. You practically raised
your siblings without your mother. Sometimes
for your mother. And you took care of her, too.'

He shook his head, and it was the terrible, tor-
mented expression stalking the darkness of his
eyes which really twisted inside her chest. Making her struggle for air.

'Tak…?'

'I wanted her dead,' he whispered at last. So
quietly that for a moment she almost missed it.

When she heard him, she didn't answer. Her
mind scrabbled around for something to say, the
right thing to say, that might possibly ease some
of that agony on his face.

But nothing came, and the more his eyes raked
over her face, wretched, bloodless, the more her
brain shut down, leaving her terrified that she
might say the wrong thing and somehow make
it worse.

In the end Effie did the only thing she could.
She reached out and took his big hand in her two
smaller ones, hating the way his body jerked as
she did so. As if he didn't trust her, when all she
wanted was to be there for him.

And then, finally, he started to speak again.
'That's why I let her push me all those years.
Why I couldn't just tell her outright to stay out
of my business and my life, to shove her idea of

an arranged marriage. I hated her, and I wanted her dead, and I've felt guilty for it all this time.'

A gurgling, maniacal laugh bubbled in her throat and it was all she could do to stuff it back down. This was all so horribly familiar.

'You think you're the only one who has wanted a parent dead?' she asked at length. 'Do you have *any* idea how many times I wished my mother would die? That she would drink herself into oblivion? Drown her failing liver until it finally gave out?'

'Well, I imagined mine might overdose on those pills of hers. Then maybe my father would come home, but I wasn't betting on it. At the very least I figured my siblings would be taken in by other members of the family. Even foster care would have been better.'

'I understand where you were coming from, but it wouldn't have been,' Effie blurted out before she could stop herself. 'You have no idea how bad it is. Plus, you'd have been split up. Your siblings ripped away from you.'

'I didn't realise that back then.' He hunched his shoulders. 'It's only since you came along and opened up to me that I've realised how good we really had it. How lucky we were not to have had *your* childhood.'

Effie shook her head. 'I'm not saying that. I would never say that. It's subjective. In some ways I only had myself to look out for. You had siblings to take care of. But then you were never alone and I was. It's different.'

'All I knew was that the more of a victim she was, the more stupid stunts she pulled to try to win him back. And the more of the monster it brought out in me.'

'You were a kid, Tak.'

'She was my *mother*.'

'She wasn't doing the job of a mother and you resented her for it. Of all people, I can understand that, Tak. Believe me. You were taking responsibility for your siblings when that wasn't supposed to be your job, and she left it to you.'

'But only because my father left *her* to do it. It should have been him I hated. Not her.'

Effie shook her head, her hollow laugh catching them both by surprise. 'It doesn't work that way. *She* was the one you trusted. The one you had expectations from. *He* wasn't. It was the same for me.'

He looked at her. Hard. As if he was trying to see right down to her very soul.

'Trust me, Tak,' she murmured softly. 'I understand where all that came from. And why.'

'Then you understand why I can't be with anyone, then. Why I would only end up hurting them, destroying them.' Bitterness leeched out of his voice, along with regret. 'Destroying *you*.'

'No. I don't see that at all.' She softened her words with a smile.

'Then you're a fool.'

'Possibly. But I think I just see the real you, whilst you're judging your childhood self on the standards of an adult. And I think you do too, or else why would you be here now?'

'I just came to apologise,' he repeated, but it lacked conviction even to his own ears.

The worst of it was that he wanted to believe her. He wanted to believe this version of himself which she claimed she knew. Of a man who might be worthy of her.

'I can't be with you.' He frowned. 'You have a daughter, responsibilities. I would only let you down and resent you for them.'

'Really? Are you sure? Only so far you haven't done either. When I needed somewhere to stay you stepped up. When I told you about Nell you asked me about her. When I confided about that shoplifting you gave me advice. It even worked—'

'You're not listening,' he broke in abruptly. But only because he'd realised he was beginning to listen to Effie and believe in her version of him.

'I *am* listening. I'm just pointing out all the ways I know you're wrong. Not to mention the peace treaty you negotiated between myself and my daughter, and the fact that you took her to that bowling alley party. You're a *good* man, Tak. You always have been.'

'I'm not,' he muttered, but it had lost more of its vehemence.

Slowly, gently, Effie bent her head forward until her forehead was pressed to his.

'Yes. You are. You fight for your family, and when you find the right woman you'll fight for her, too.'

And she said it with such certainty, such ferocity, that Tak felt all his walls beginning to tumble, stone block by stone block. As if her love was a wrecking ball which could topple even the best-built defences.

Love.

The word jolted him. Did she love him? Did he love her?

Possibly, he realised with a start. Perhaps he had even from that first night.

'I've already found her,' he heard himself say instead.

And then, because he didn't know what more to say, he did the only thing he could think of to do.

He snaked his hand up to the back of her neck, tilting her head until their mouths fitted together as though it had been inevitable from the very start of their conversation.

He poured everything he had into that single kiss. As if it would convey all the thoughts he couldn't articulate. As if it would make every word she was saying about him come true.

It was a kiss which went far deeper than anything he could have said, and it might have gone on for an entire eternity. Maybe two.

But it didn't. Ultimately it had to end.

'I didn't mean to do that.' He only half apologised as he lifted his mouth from hers. 'I tried to walk away, Effie. But I couldn't. There's this dark…*thing* which twists and knots inside me. I don't expect anything from you. I came to tell you that I should have told you the truth from the start. And that I'm sorry I didn't.'

It hurt. So very badly.

'Yes.'

She sounded composed, but he could see the vein pulsing at her neck. A fraction too fast. Too fluttery.

'You *should* have told me that you were using me not simply as a buffer but to shock your family into leaving you alone. You should have been clear that you weren't inviting me to stay because you were worried about Nell and I not having a roof over our heads but because you wanted the dramatic vision of an unmarried single mother being your lover.'

'That's not entirely accurate. I invited you and Nell to stay because I couldn't stand by and watch you live in that flat,' he asserted. 'But once I realised the visual it was creating for the more traditionalist side of my family I admit I played up to it.'

'What about the dates? And taking Nell to that birthday party?'

'I took Nell because she needed the opportunity to go and meet new friends and you were working.'

'But the dating?'

'Yes…' He paused, not even sure himself. 'And no.'

'What about Paris?'

He exhaled heavily. 'I couldn't believe you'd never been out of the country before. I loved the idea of being the person to take you abroad for the first time. But I admit there was also a part of me that knew it would get back to my family and keep things stirred up.'

She nodded, as though she was grateful for his honesty. As though every single word he uttered wasn't rushing into her, pouring into her chest and stinging her heart and stopping it, the way a swarm of bees might kill an enemy one tiny sting at a time. Individually merely painful but combined ultimately fatal.

The way it felt for him.

'Why did you love the idea of taking me abroad?' she managed at last.

Tak fought to gather his thoughts. It wasn't an action he'd had to take before. 'I told you—you got under my skin in a way no one has ever done before. I didn't know what to do with it. It's how things became so confused.'

'I could have forgiven you all of that,' she whispered. 'If you hadn't been intimate with me.'

'Ah…' For the first time in a while that heady,

intoxicating glint was reignited in his eyes. He could feel it. 'Now *that*, I can say with absolute honesty, was never part of the plan.'

She stared at him for a long, long moment, and time seemed to stand still. 'Never?'

That flash of hope in her eyes did things to him that he couldn't even understand, let alone explain.

'No, intimacy was never my intention,' he told her honestly. That was simply me finding myself unable to resist you.'

'You couldn't resist me?' Effie was trying to sound sceptical. Worldly.

Tak managed not to grin in triumph. 'How could I?' he murmured. 'Since I'd managed to fall for you.'

Her reaction was all he could have hoped for. From the shallow breathing to the shift in her body language, and from the quickened pulse to the way her all too expressive eyes betrayed her.

'You…you fell for me?'

'I'm in love with you, Effie.'

The words came out on their own. Yet they felt as right and as true as anything ever had.

'Surely you know that? Even if you don't trust me with your head, let your heart answer this one. I love you—and there's no game-play, no agenda. You're the one who broke through to me when I thought it was impossible for anyone to reach me. You're the one who made me finally see that, time and again, I was giving my mother the benefit of the doubt because of all that she'd been through with my father and with Saaj, but she was never going to be the woman or the mother I wanted her to be.'

He spoke as though it was a fact—like his lungs fuelling him with oxygen, or his heart pumping blood around his body. Not that either of them seemed to be functioning normally right now. They seemed to flip-flop between working too hard and forgetting to work at all.

Tak shook his head gently and lifted his palms to cup her face. 'You doubt it?'

She finally found her tongue, ready to counter him as she so often had. But this time her voice was full of awe, incredulity.

'How could I possibly have known? You never once even suggested it.'

'On the contrary...' He dragged his finger over her bottom lip, his eyes following the movement as if spellbound. 'I may not have said the words but I betrayed myself time and again every time I worshipped your body.'

'That was merely sex—'

Her voice was raspy, bumpy. But then, so was his.

'We both know that it was never *merely* sex.'

If only he'd allowed himself to admit that much, much earlier.

'Still, you can't just walk away from your family, Tak. I know how much your siblings mean to you.'

He had to concentrate. Answer her every question. But he was having a hard time not simply bending his head and claiming her again.

'Hetti is in despair,' he muttered, struggling to drag his gaze from those luscious lips of hers. 'She wants you to know how desperately sorry she is. She has no idea how my mother got hold of her key but she is adamant that she didn't give it to her. And Sasha has long since said she can do without the drama. She's trying to concentrate on her own family and she doesn't want them being dragged into that life. As for Rafi—he has loathed both our parents ever since he could talk. I don't think there's any chance of any of them being upset that I've finally decided to cut all ties.'

'It all sounds too perfect, too easy,' Effie vacillated. 'But I don't just have myself to think about. I have Nell. And, as ever, the idea of doing something which could end up harming my daughter in some way is something I refuse to even entertain.'

'I *know* how important Nell is,' he confirmed.

'I want to believe you,' Effie choked out. 'But love…it's a big deal.'

And then he gave up trying to fight his instincts any longer.

'I love you, Effie. And every time I tell you I only become more and more certain of that fact.'

'I want to believe you…'

'I know,' he murmured, lowering his mouth to hers again. 'I know that it's just been you and Nell for so long. I know that with everything you've been through in your life that you've never loved or trusted anyone else this way. But it's time to take that risk, Effie.'

'Tak…'

'Stop over-analysing,' he murmured softly. 'I love you, Effie. I'm *in* love with you. Let me prove it to you. Let me spend the rest of my life proving it to you.'

And then he claimed her mouth and set about honouring his word in the best way he knew how.

EPILOGUE

It was almost three years later to the day when Tak found himself staring at the 4D image of his new baby, who yawned widely before defiantly turning his back on them. It took everything Tak had to tear his gaze from the screen and down to his wife of eighteen months who, impossibly, appeared more beautiful to him with every passing day.

'It's incredible...' he breathed.

'Incredible,' Effie echoed, her hands instinctively reaching for his.

'Nell is going to be livid she missed this,' he smiled. 'Her new baby brother.'

'I promised her we'd watch the video with her as many times as she wants to as soon as she gets home from her exchange trip. Our family.'

Our family. Happiness spiralled through him. His baby, his wife and his stepdaughter—who, at sixteen, was beginning to exert her independence more and more.

Nell was going to be as stunning as her mother, and Tak could imagine the trail of broken-hearted young men she was going to leave in her wake. He might only just have become her stepfather, but he felt honoured that she had accepted him into her life as if he was the real father she'd never had. She had even tagged his name onto her own, just as Effie had.

'We have a new addition to our family, Mrs Robinson-Basu,' he whispered, awe flowing throughout his body.

'We do!' Her eyes shone brightly—too brightly.

'More tears of joy?' He laughed. 'You're turning into quite the mushy little thing, aren't you?'

'Shut up,' she chastised him with a laugh. 'And just be glad that I love you as much as I do, Tak Basu.'

'You do, huh?' he teased her, never tiring of hearing her say those words.

'I do,' she confirmed. 'I love you.'

'And I love you too.' He dropped a kiss on her lips, then on her stomach. 'And I love *you*, little one. With all my heart.'

* * * * *

If you enjoyed this story, check out these other great reads from Charlotte Hawkes

Christmas with Her Bodyguard
The Surgeon's One-Night Baby
A Bride to Redeem Him
Tempted by Dr. Off-Limits

All available now!